YELLOWHAWK

Books of Poetry
by Jane Stuart

A YEAR'S HARVEST
EYES OF THE MOLE
WHITE BARN

YELLOWHAWK

Jane Stuart

McGRAW-HILL BOOK COMPANY
New York   St. Louis   San Francisco
Düsseldorf   London   Mexico   Sydney   Toronto

We acknowledge gratefully permissions received to include the stories which were originally published as follows:

"This Business of Roses," © 1970, *Green River Review*.

"The Spirits of Hood's Run," © *Kansas Magazine,* 1964, and "The Cup Shall Pass to Thee," © *Kansas Quarterly,* Winter 1969–70, II, 1, are reprinted with the permission of their respective publishers.

"Vianella," © *Arizona Quarterly,* Autumn 1964, Vol. XX, No. 3, and "Playing Possum," © *Arizona Quarterly,* Winter 1974, Vol. XXVI, No. 4.

23456789 BPBP 79876543

Library of Congress Cataloging in Publication Data
Stuart, Jane.
Yellowhawk.
I. Title.
PZ4.S927Ye [PS3569.T82] 813'.5'4 72–10001
ISBN 0–07–062196–9

To Julian

✤FOREWORD✤

I have been teaching at Yellowhawk for six years now and I've never regretted a minute of it. The most important decision I ever made was on that rainy day when I went ahead and drove myself down the river road into a new world. It was raining on the first Tuesday after Labor Day and I hate to drive in the rain. I'm afraid I'll lose control of the car again and go off the road, over the bank, and into the Ohio River. It's happened before, and I keep asking myself why shouldn't it happen to me? Why not me this time? I know this isn't a positive way to think and I shouldn't let my thoughts go out of control that way, but I couldn't help myself. I'm a poor driver and I hate to be out on the roads when it's raining.

But it was the first Tuesday after Labor Day and I couldn't make any excuses for not showing up at work. I had to drive to Yellowhawk and meet Mr. Jenkins, the principal there, and start in on my first day of schoolteaching. I had to meet the other teachers and I had to see my students and let them look me over. I haven't been out of school long enough to forget what the first day is for. You go early to look the teacher over and pick out your seat. If you're lucky and the teacher likes you, she won't move you. When I was in the sixth grade I got to school at seven-thirty on the first day and picked out the seat closest to the door so I could be the first one out at lunchtime and recess. But the teacher said I talked too much there and she moved me to the third row, even though I'd gotten there at seven-thirty in the morning.

To get to Yellowhawk from my house you drive off the ridge, out of the valley, and get on the main road that follows the river down past Lloyd, almost all the way to South Line and the bridge that leads to Ohio. It's a long drive and when it's raining, the roads get slippery and seem to have twice as many curves. When I first started out, I wondered what I'd gotten myself into, making a drive like that twice a day. But after that first day I didn't think any more about it because it wasn't important and I realized that I couldn't go on living my life thinking that death was always waiting around every curve or corner. After that first day at Yellowhawk, I understood a little more about people. I understood that life is very important and when you become an important part of an important world, you think you're going to live forever and you want to, no matter what's behind you.

As I drove along, the mist was rising on the Ohio River and I could hear boats horning and whistling in the early-morning darkness. I felt like I was going into another world as I watched the first lights come on in some of the houses along the way. I wondered who lived here and what they thought about when they first got up and started getting ready to meet another day. And I wondered if any of these people would be coming to Yellowhawk and, if they did, would I get to know them and how would we get on together.

Yellowhawk school is a new red-brick elementary school sprawled ranch style along the flat river land that curves up to meet the hills behind it. It looks like all the other eastern-Kentucky elementary schools built ten or fifteen years ago because they were all built alike. But it isn't like any other school because each school is different. The students and teachers are different, and each school makes up a world of its own. Children laugh at different jokes and cry over different hurts. The teachers come in yawning and sleepy after getting their own families off to work or school and when they go inside their classrooms they teach geography or math or history the way they see it or the way they were taught. The things that should make us all alike make us different, and for the first time in my life I saw how much other people were like me, and yet how different.

Mr. Jenkins was waiting for me in his office. His wife was sitting beside him at the desk, chewing gum and talking to the other teachers and the cook who had just plugged in a big pot of coffee. No one said anything when I walked in the room; no one offered to shake hands or even leave so that I could talk to Mr.

Jenkins in private. At first I didn't know what to do. I felt strange and embarrassed and I hoped he wasn't going to let on if he knew the real reasons that I had come here to work.

"Well, Rhoda Miller," he said, not standing up, not offering to shake hands or pull up a chair for me, "it's good you're here. We've been waiting for you."

I felt my face turn red because it was only seven-fifteen and I was the last one to arrive.

"We don't always get here so early," he said, laughing as he unwrapped a stick of Juicy-Fruit gum and popped it into his mouth. "Just the first day of school—I like to make sure all my teachers are going to show up."

Then he laughed again and I watched his face crinkle up with wrinkles.

"Go on, sit down," he said. "Have a cup of coffee and I'll tell you a little bit about what goes on at Yellowhawk."

I listened, drinking a cup of coffee and then smoking a cigarette, standing in Mr. Jenkins' bathroom so the students passing by the principal's office couldn't see.

When I walked into the eighth-grade classroom at eight-thirty, I was ready to go. I felt as if I'd been teaching there at Yellowhawk for years. I knew every teacher and most of the students. And what I didn't know I knew I'd soon find out. It was going to be the same for me, too, I realized. What they didn't know about Rhoda Miller or couldn't guess they would find out by asking around. But I wasn't going to be ashamed and I wasn't going to care. I had been looking for a new life and I'd found it.

Now I have married again and had to quit teaching because my first baby is due in three months. Mr. Jenkins let me stay on as long as he could, but at last the time came when the school board knew and there would have been trouble if Yellowhawk hadn't let me go.

Some day, when my children are grown and in school themselves, I want to go back to Yellowhawk and teach the eighth grade again. People always say that it's a mistake to try to live your life over again, but I don't think it would be a mistake to go back to Yellowhawk. It might not be the same but it couldn't be very different. Places like that can never really change because they don't give way to the coldness and nothingness that turn men away from the world and God to look inside themselves for all the answers. A place like Yellowhawk will stay free and happy because Yellowhawk people can look at themselves and smile or cry but still accept the world for what it is and not judge it for what it ought to be.

❧ I ❧

When the roads were muddy and ugly with deep rutted gashes that thawing water flowed over and wedged deeper into spring earth, Rosalina Scaggs wore an old pair of black loafers down the hollow. She carried her good shoes in a paper bag, up in her arms with her schoolbooks. And she stood alone, hunched under a thick-branched tree to break the wind, as she waited for the schoolbus. She waited a long time, usually half an hour. The bus driver always came at seven-thirty, but Rosalina was there by seven o'clock. She was afraid that someday the bus would be early and she would miss her ride. The thoughts of being left in the country for a day terrified Rosalina. She lay awake in bed each morning, long before she stretched her bare feet out from beneath the comforter to grope for the small hand-made rug on the cold wood floor. She lay there, her tiny head sunk deep into the feather pillow, wondering what would happen to her if she ever missed the schoolbus.

"They'd come for me from school," she thought. But she knew they wouldn't. They'd only think she was sick, and send back a note by one of her children. The note wouldn't reach her until after five o'clock. Dark would have fallen. The moon would be slinking along behind those black witch trees, goggling down on her alone in the old house.

"What'd I do?" Rosalina wondered. "What'd I do here alone all day, with them watching me?" Her black eyes rolled in terror from one side of the room to the other. She stared at the wall paper, making sure it was still flat and unbroken planes of green and gray stripes; at the windows, to see if in the night they had been pried open. They could get her, here on the second floor, she knew. They could skimmy up the walls if they wanted, or break through at the windows. And she would jump from her bed, throwing on a heavy robe, and run to the kitchen to heat water for her coffee.

In the mornings, the kitchen of the old house was less gloomy, with the sunlight streaking feebly through the cracks in the door and the dirty panes of window glass. So Rosalina stood by the stove to strip off her robe and muslin gown and wash herself in the washpan. She kept her closet in the kitchen too, because she felt it was safest to dress here.

"They're afraid of fire," she told herself. "I could throw a stick or two of flaming kindling at them. They'd run then!" So she kept a poker propped against the stove. That way, if she ever needed to rake out the burning wood in a hurry, she could.

"My, my, you look cold," the bus driver told her, as he flung open the screechy yellow doors to let her on. "You must have got here early this morning."

"I did, I did," Rosalina told him, ducking her head nervously as she took her seat behind the driver. "I was up early this morning."

"A lot to do, huh, living up here alone?"

"Yes, a lot to do."

"Don't you ever get scared, being by yourself?"

"Sometimes, sometimes," Rosalina said, and hastily opened a book. The driver gave her bad nerves.

He seemed to be laughing at her, seemed to know why she clamored on the bus, stiff with terror and cold, each morning. He sensed her fear, and laughed at her. "It's not funny," she told herself. "It's not funny. If he lived up there, the way I do, he'd be scared, too. Uh-huh. He'd be afraid of them."

"You might as well talk to me awhile, Miss Scaggs," said the driver. "We got a long way to go before we get the next ones."

"Yes," Rosalina said, "there's a long piece in-between."

"How come you stay up there by yourself, Miss Scaggs?" the driver asked, looking at her slyly through the rear-view mirror.

"It's my home," Rosalina snapped. "I've lived there all my life."

"Oh."

Then he said, "Aren't you afraid to live by yourself?"

"I told you, sometimes."

The driver smiled at having riled her so, and went back to concentrating on skirting the deep ruts in the road.

The next stop came at the farmhouse where Rosalina's parents and children lived.

"Hello, Miss Scaggs," Braddley said politely, climbing on the bus.

"Good morning, Braddley."

"Hello, Miss Scaggs," Kay and Wolfe smiled shyly.

"Hello."

"Good morning, Miss Scaggs," Margaret said embarrassedly, and hurried to the back of the bus.

"Good morning, Margaret," Rosalina said to the gust of wind that remained in place of her daughter.

The children settled themselves into empty seats and waved good-by to their grandmother, who was waving to them from the front door.

Rosalina gave no sign of recognition to her mother.

The bus driver shook his head and drove on.

Rosalina was very proper about her relationship with her children. Since she was the supervisor of the Egg-Hollow bus, she considered herself officially on duty at seven-thirty when she boarded. At four-fifteen, when all the passengers except the children and herself had been let off, she relaxed and spoke more intimately with them.

"It's silly, how you carry on with them, Rosalina," Principal Jenkins often chided.

"It's not silly," Rosalina would say stubbornly.

"Yes, it is," Jenkins argued, chewing hard on his gum. "Almost every teacher here at Yellowhawk has a child in the school. And that child calls her Mommy. But you make yours call you Miss Scaggs. It's silly."

"When I'm teaching," Rosalina said, "I am Miss Scaggs. To everyone. Not Mommy to some, and teacher to others. No, sir, that's what's not right."

Principal Jenkins shook his head, and waved Rosalina off. She was set in her ways. She was strange.

"I'm not strange," Rosalina thought, thumbing through the

second-grade teaching book. "I do what I think is right." And she thought no more about it.

From the back of the bus, Margaret stared at her mother's small head, smaller and rounder looking because of the short thick black hair she kept slicked down smooth against it. Being in the same school with her was hard for Margaret. She was embarrassed when she met Miss Scaggs in the hall or the restroom or the principal's office. Mr. Jenkins had told her that she must not worry, must not feel this way—that she must accept her mother as her mother wanted, as Miss Scaggs in the daytime and Mother at night.

But it wasn't easy for Margaret to do this. She was an eighth grader now, and sensitive about the strange life she and her family led. Her schoolmates, who had heard their parents talk about the situation and knew not to ask any questions, were not really interested in Margaret's home problems. Not even Braddley or Kay or Wolfe seemed to mind not living with their mother, or knowing who their father was, or seeing how funny everybody else thought Miss Scaggs was.

"Well, it may not be too bad now," Margaret had once said to Mr. Jenkins," but what's it going to be like next year when I go to high school? I'll have to fill out forms then. It's all right to put I live with my grandparents, but what'll I say about Daddy? Mommy won't tell us who he is and says we're never to ask her or talk about it. And she won't talk about the rest of us..."

Lester Jenkins, who was sympathetic to Margaret's problems but a very busy man, usually shooed the girl from his office with a promise of seeing her about it later or speaking with Possum Arthur, the high school principal, so she need not worry. "After all," he said to himself, "what can I do for the girl? I can't tell her the things her mother doesn't want her to know, now, can I?"

Once at school, Rosalina would go quickly to the teacher's restroom where she washed her face, hands, and feet, and scrubbed her shoes clean of the heavy mud that was clinging to them.

"There's no need to scrape and rub so, Rosalina," Zania France had once said to her. "You'll just dirty them up walking home tonight."

But Rosalina scrubbed on. "They won't catch me with my shoes dirty," she told herself. "Never, never."

The cooks kept pots of hot coffee made for the teachers, so Rosalina had something else warm in her stomach before she began the day. If she were hungry, she would buy a candy bar from the office supply, or take whatever had been left over from the previous day's luncheon. The cooks were used to Rosalina's ways, and never crossed her. She was scrupulously honest with them—she had never cheated them out of the price of a cup of coffee or a piece of leftover apple pie.

Kay and Wolfe were in Rosalina's class. They seemed oblivious to the fact that their mother taught them. They called her Miss Scaggs as readily as the others, and seemed to hesitate only when it was afternoon, and they were told to call her Mommy. Mommy and Grandmommy and Miss Scaggs were very confused in their minds.

At the noon hour, when she had playground duty, Rosalina stood as close to the children as she could. If one came up to her and took her hand, she was grateful for the warmth of the little fingers squeezing her own so tightly. She supervised the games fiercely, watching every movement to detect any unfair play or prevent any child straying too far from the others. "Then I'd have to go after him," she realized. "I'd have to cross that wide field by myself. Who knows, they might be waiting for me in the grass. They might snag my heels as I walked through. Oh Lord, Lord."

"Sometimes," she thought, "I wouldn't go after one, even if he only ran across the creek. I'd send a big boy. One of the seventh graders." So she tried to steer her class as close to the seventh graders as she could. But she knew that this wouldn't work. The big boys were too engrossed with their baseball games to go after a little one. "I'd have to go alone," Rosalina thought, terrified. "Alone."

She looked at her second graders with fear. "How I love them," she thought. "They are soft and warm and little and unafraid. They don't know about the ones who are waiting for them. They don't know about what will happen to them when they grow up."

She wished that she knew enough magic to make the children stay this way forever.

Once Margaret had crawled on Rosalina's lap and said, "Mommy, where did I come from?"

Not at all taken aback, Rosalina replied, "Why from a rose, dear."

"A rose?"

"Yes. It opened up its white petals and you fell out into my lap."

"Oh." Margaret, satisfied with this explanation, had thought nothing else about it until years later, when her grandmother told her the truth. Then she had felt hurt that her mother had deceived her, and refused to share the truth. Later on, though, she began to wonder if perhaps her mother didn't believe that this business of roses was really true. "My mother," Margaret realized, unhappily, "is a strange woman."

That evening Rosalina said good-by to Margaret, Braddley, Kay, and Wolfe at her mother's house. She watched them climb off the bus and run for the big white farmhouse and the fresh milk and cookies waiting for them.

"They're better off there," Rosalina thought. "They live in a warm, safe house. They have each other. And they don't have to worry about—anything—harming them. Someday maybe I can go to live with them, too. But I can't go now, not when there's the danger of—being followed."

The trek up the Egg-Hollow hill was steep and slushy. Rosalina's old black loafers kicked up gobs of mud and soft grass. The trees, violent black prisoners marching against the sky, waved their chain branches at her as if to cry out, "Join us or set us free." And the sun, their guard against evil spirits who set upon them and plucked at their leafy fatness, sank flaming into the deep well of hill slopes, leaving the road and Rosalina chilly and deserted. Shadows leapt in all directions, as the wind blew tauntingly through whistling rocks. The creek, croaking and spitting as it roared downstream with its load of winter debris, was wild music to Rosalina's ears, wild chants of wickedness pulsating madly to the tune of the wind against her back.

"Oh, Lord," Rosalina sighed. "It's going to be a hard night."

The house was dark and cold. It's crooked etching against the skyline, caused by the foundations settling unevenly, formed a toothy grin to the lone woman approaching. Rosalina took the key from her purse and unlocked the door. It swung open and knocked against the wall with a fierce hammering wail. Immediately, she switched on the lights and lit the stove. Flames dancing through the chilly air revived her, and she poured a panful of water to heat.

A jet soared overhead, causing the windows to rattle. Rosalina jumped and spilled some cream she was carrying to the table. "What's happening tonight?" she wondered. "What's going on out there?"

She checked to make sure the door was bolted.

"I don't guess it makes too much difference," she said to herself. "If they want in, they'll come anyway. Locked doors won't keep them out."

Once again, she wished her children were with her. It would be comforting to see little Wolfe and Kay playing with their crayons and paper. But it was a selfish wish, to endanger the lives of her children, to give the other a chance to cast their spells on four innocents.

"If only we were all roses," Rosalina thought dreamily. "White roses, blooming in the moonlight and drowsing in the sun, our petals beautiful but untouchable. We would not be men and women, subject to evil, sinning against our own beauty. Only white roses blowing in the wind. Birth would be painless and death a sinking into the warm sweet earth." She shook her head, and wiped away a tear on her blouse sleeve.

"But we're not," she sighed. "We're only ugly men and women, whose seeds bear ugliness and bitterness and misunderstanding."

It began to rain. The chimney choked and spat back fire before the spitting embers wheezed and buried themselves in the ashes on the hearth. A charred log rolled out onto the floor. Strong gusts of wind broke the frail door latch, and banged the door hard against the wall. Rosalina, immobile and mute with terror, sat clenching her fists in her lap, her small head bent over the oil-cloth-covered table.

"They're coming for me," she thought quietly. "At last, they're coming for me. Orville? Orville?" The word, ugly and rasping to her tongue, fell from its hiding place of years. "Orville?"

The wind, dancing freely through the room, blew her robe from its pin on the door across a kitchen chair.

"Orville, why have you waited so long?" Rosalina asked with no feeling in her voice. "I've been ready for you. I knew you were coming."

The robe slumping over the table did not answer.

"Tell me, Orville," Rosalina touched a sleeve timidly. Her black eyes were narrowed and inquisitive; she was searching for the hands and the face of this spirit who was facing her. "I've been haunted for years," she went on, her mouth flopping open and shut mechanically as if she had no control over it. "I've been paying for a sin. At first I didn't think I should, and I fought hard. It wasn't my fault about the smokehouse catching on fire, Orville. I fought hard to save you and the others. I burned my feet and my hands. I burned my hair. My eyes got filled with smoke, and I couldn't see. I could hear you in there. I could hear you and Kate and Timothy. I know you needed me. And I tried to get there."

Rosalina's mouth was dry. Her lips were moving, but no sound came. She was no longer addressing anything in the room, only the spirits who had come for her in her mind. "It was hard to lose a husband and two children, Orville. Even though the children were not mine. Even though you didn't belong to me. It was hard."

"What do you want me to do, Orville?" she said. "I've tried awful hard. I've raised your family." Her face, now drenched with the heavy rain slapping in from the storm outside, was turned blankly to the wall. Little trickles of water began to flow across the floor, wetting her feet. She did not move.

Flash flood, the wind beat out the words against the roof of the house. Flash flood.

The creeks were overflowing, ripping out of their crusty banks and surging across the muddy fields. Trees, caught up in the vortex of winds gone wild with thunder and lightning and rain, smashed their way against each other as they sought a place to fall. The moon, soaked out of the sky, tipped her head above Egg

Hollow and let out the water that was damming up her ears. Down it came, into the chimney, into the hearth's scorched ashes.

The hills themselves began to shake and quiver, rumbling ominously that this outrage of a spring night was too much for their gentle slopes to bear. Rosalina felt the wood foundations of the house begin to give. Beneath her, the wood broke and crumbled and slid across the slick slimy hill; above her, the patched-up roof, sucked up by the suction of wind and trees and storm, began to tear loose. Flash flood, the stove coughed, as it slid across the linoleum floor and battered through the wall.

The house, gathering momentum, rolled and rocked as it crashed its way down the steep hill, scattering the debris of furniture and clothes and thoughts and fears into the storm, tearing up by their roots the wild roses blooming in its path.

❧ II ❧

"Joy to the world, Miss Savage, Joy to the world, Mommy's had a little boy, and I have a brother. Joy to the world, Miss Savage, Jesus has sent us a son and I won't be lonely no more." Tullie ran skipping through the field of daisies and dandelions, running her bare thin feet across the cold spring grass and making her toes wriggle each blade she could catch between them.

"Joy, joy, Miss Savage. Daddy's coming home to see my brother Ed. Maybe he'll be so happy now that he will stay with us. Maybe we're going to be a storybook family after all."

Tullie ran up and down the field, zigzagging her way through the neat rows of flowers that the wind had sewn in the green spring meadow. Her bare feet ran skipping, her cold legs hurried behind them, faster and faster, hurrying to keep up with the narrow feet that slid and skipped across the early March grass.

> On my way from Easter Gap,
> On my way to see my pap,
> Going home to my brother Ed,
> Fast asleep in my mommy's bed.

Tullie sang and danced in the meadow until, tired, she flopped down beside the brown fallen tree that lay across a dry creekbed and marked, in Tullie's mind, the boundaries between her meadow and the land that lay beyond.

She lay on her back, her face turned up to the sky, counting kittens and dogs that tumbled by in the white somersaulting clouds. Oh wonder day, she thought, when the little boy Jesus put the kitten and dogs that have died on earth up in the clouds. Now I can watch them go by, and I can be happy because I know that they are.

"No, he's not, no he's not, brown baron," she said suddenly to the wind in passing. "My little dog's not drowned and lying in the bottom of the Sandy River. My daddy didn't drown my dog and drop him there. My doggie ran away, the night before Christmas, and the little boy Jesus found him and put him in the clouds. He's up there now, chasing cats and looking for me." Tullie lay on the cold ground and watched the sky, her fingers grabbing for acorns and prodding them into the still hard ground.

Then she heard the school bell ringing. Far away, the bell was ringing to tell her that she must hurry, or she would be late again. Late to school, late to Miss Savage's classroom, late to the boys and girls who stared at her and frightened her and made her lose her voice and forget what she had to say. Late to watch them looking at her, laughing at her, making fun of her behind her back, or sometimes, when Miss Savage wasn't watching, to her face.

"Lord, Lord, I have to run," she said. She leaped from the ground and began her zigzag dance across the dry creekbed, leaving her meadow, crossing to the land that lay beyond.

Down the hill she went, fast as the wind, brown-baron wind that was following her, puffing, hurrying to keep up with her slim feet and long lean legs. Laughing and crying to herself at once, as she thought about Mommy at home in bed with her new brother Ed, her secret, her own secret come true. Laughing and crying as she thought about Daddy over in Carson, sure to hear the news and come home to see them all.

It's not Christmas now, Daddy, you don't have to bring us no presents, she thought. Just come and see us. Just come.

As she neared the slope of the hill, she stopped running and began to walk. Her walk was slow, her right foot twisted in the grass and fell limp, dragging itself along behind her left foot. In her mind, she could hear them already, saying to each other, "Here comes Tullie, late and lame! Tullie, Tullie, that's her name!" She tried to stand tall but her shoulders began to crimp, and she could not pull herself up straight. So she walked slowly, hunched forward, the right foot twisting itself behind the left that struggled to make a way through the stubbled grass.

"Come recess today and I am going to play," she said, as she neared the school. "I am going to play Red Rover and I am going to run so hard and throw myself at them with all my strength. I'll break Priscilla's arm, I'll hit her so hard. I'll make her scream. Then she won't say nothing to me again."

Miss Savage said, as she came in the room, "You're late again, Tullie."

Tullie bowed her head, said nothing, and slipped into her seat in the back row.

"Do you want lunch?"

Tullie kept her head down low, and nodded only once. It was her sign to Miss Savage. Miss Savage knew the sign, and she made a checkmark by Tullie's name on the lunch list.

"You've got to pay," the boy in front of her said, under his breath.

"I've got no money," Tullie snapped.

"See, Miss Savage, she can talk," Bill Bowen said. "She can talk, I heard her."

"That will be enough, Bill," Miss Savage said. She went to the blackboard and continued writing out arithmetic problems. "Copy these on your papers, and begin to work them," she said, her back still to the class.

Priscilla Mayhew turned around from her seat in the front row and stuck out her tongue at Tullie.

"Stop it, stop it, stop it," Tullie said under her breath. "I'll break your arm if you don't."

She made a face back, turning her mouth down at the corners and crossing her eyes at Priscilla.

"Ooh, Miss Savage," Priscilla screamed, jumping up as if Bill Bowen had left a tack on her seat. "She put a hex on me. I saw her."

Miss Savage faced the class. "Priscilla, what are you talking about?"

"Tullie Cameron. I saw her do it. She's putting a hex on me. She's got the devil's eye, and she's making it work on me."

"Priscilla!" Miss Savage said. "That will be enough."

"But Miss Savage..."

"Priscilla, one more word from you and I am going to take you to the principal's office. Now sit facing the blackboard and do your arithmetic."

Priscilla took up her pencil and began to copy down the addition and subtraction. But she couldn't concentrate. She felt Tullie's hex crawling up and down her neck, she felt the devil's eye sneaking under the collar of her dress. Her mind wouldn't work. She couldn't add, she couldn't subtract. She couldn't hold the pencil upright, and the paper kept slipping out from under her hand.

In the back seat, Tullie held the tip of her own pencil on her tongue and stared at the board, trying to make out what the numbers were.

Bill Bowen moved aside so that Tullie could copy from his paper.

"You did very well today, Tullie," Miss Savage said, when she came around to check their answers. "You have been studying, haven't you?"

Tullie ducked her head down between her shoulders and grinned into the wood of the desk.

Then there was a knock on the door and Pam Braden who sat in the chair by the door today because it was her turn to answer it, jumped up and almost stumbled across her feet in her hurry to yank the door open.

"Principal's office," said a big eighth grader.

"Miss Savage," Pam squeaked, "Miss Savage."

Miss Savage came to the door. "Yes?" And she took the note from the big eighth grader's hand that was stretched out like an evil paw to hand over its evil message.

"Straight from the devil," Tullie thought.

Miss Savage sighed. "Tullie, could I speak to you in the hall?" she said.

Tullie pulled herself out of her seat, slowly, the second time Miss Savage spoke to her, and limped toward the door.

"I told you you were going to get it," Priscilla hissed as she went out.

As she pulled the door shut, Tullie grinned wildly at Priscilla

Mayhew, showing the inside of her mouth, half empty of teeth, full of pink swollen gums.

"Ooh," Priscilla said. "She's done it again."

The class tittered.

"Tullie," Miss Savage said, when the door was shut and there was no one else in the hall. "Tullie," and the hall was quiet and black, no lights, no sounds of feet shuffling or children coughing as they opened and closed their books. "I have a note from the principal's office. You went down to the third grade yesterday afternoon, didn't you?"

She said nothing.

"Didn't you, Tullie? Don't you remember? I said you could go, in the afternoon, to sit with the little ones and listen to the stories."

"Yes, yes, yes, I went."

Miss Savage sighed. "Tullie, Miss Longer says her watch is missing and that some of the children say you took it. Is that true?"

The hall was black and quiet, silent, dark, no voices, no joy, no little boy Jesus sitting there to watch. And listen.

No, no, Miss Savage, you know I wouldn't do nothing like that, she said to herself. You know I'm not that kind of person. I'm a good girl, Miss Savage, I'm good and they say awful things about me because they don't like me and they tell their kids not to have anything to do with me. So they say awful things about me and try to hurt me so I'll go away and never come back.

"Tullie, are you listening?"

Tullie nodded.

"Tullie, do you know anything about the watch?"

"No."

"All right. Shall we go down and talk with Miss Longer?"

I don't want to go there. I don't want to go down there and have them all laughing at me. They don't like me. They took the watch and put it in my shoe. When I wasn't looking. They put it there, when one of them was sitting on my lap and the other had her hands over my eyes and another one was holding my arms behind me. I couldn't help it. But I didn't take the watch. I'm not that kind of person.

"Shall we go, Tullie?"

"No."

"Then will you go and get the watch?"

Tullie limped back inside the room, back to her desk in the end row. She leaned down and looked into the black hole of her desk, she stuck her hand into the big square beehive and prodded among the books and wads of storybook paper. Then she squatted on the floor and reached again, working her fingers through the paper until she came upon the little wad that held the watch. She took out the watch, wrapped in a square of red construction paper, folded neatly, and stuck it into her arithmetic book.

"Tullie's going to be in a match," Bill Bowen whispered, and everyone laughed.

She hurried back to the door, her face on fire, limping as fast as she could go, her heart thumping under the thin cotton of her dress. "Here," she said, and stuck the book at Miss Savage. "Here, take it."

Miss Savage opened the book and took out the watch. It was still running.

"Why did you take it?"

"Didn't take it."

"I'll have to talk to the principal, Tullie."

Tullie bowed her head.

"Do you want to wait for me inside, or come along?"

Tullie hurried back to her seat, folded her arms on her desk, put down her head, and cried. No one in the room said anything. Her classmates sat very still, very quiet, listening to Tullie's sobs. Pam Braden sat up tall in her chair, pencil and tablet on her desk. She was to take the names of anyone who talked while Miss Savage was out of the room.

"Don't cry, Tullie," Bill Bowen whispered, looking straight ahead of him so that Pam Braden wouldn't be able to see him turned around, and catch him talking. "Don't cry."

Tullie sobbed louder. Her classmates shuffled their feet under their desks and opened and closed their books. Then Priscilla Mayhew got out of her seat and walked back to the back of the room, with a book to put in her locker. She stopped behind

Tullie's desk and put her hand on Tullie's shoulder. "Don't cry, Tullie," she whispered. "It'll be all right. I know it will. Please don't cry. We won't tease you any more."

"Ooh," Tullie cried aloud.

"You can play with us at recess." It was all that Priscilla could say.

It was everything that Tullie wanted. She stopped her crying, wiped her red swollen eyes with an arm, and smiled at Priscilla. Seeing her smile that way, with her mouth open, frightened Priscilla, who remembered what her mother had said about not talking to Tullie or she might catch whatever it was that Tullie had.

Miss Savage came back into the room and erased the board. It was time for spelling. They began to copy their spelling words onto their lined tablet paper, and the bell rang.

"First row line up," Pam Braden said.

The first row scrambled to its feet and formed a straight line at the door.

"Second row," Pam Braden called. "Third, fourth, and fifth rows."

Then Miss Savage opened the door and the long neat line went quietly down the hall, breaking as the big door was opened and boys and girls spilled out into the yard, heading for swings, slides, baseball, and a big empty field where a game of Red Rover was already being started by the fifth graders who fled when they saw the sixth grade thundering out behind Priscilla Mayhew.

The third time around, somebody called Red Rover, Red Rover, send Tullie right over.

Tullie grinned and hid her face behind her arm.

"Go on, Tullie," Jo Ann Jackson said. "Go on."

"Can't."

"Don't push her, Jo Ann," William Sizemore said. "You know she can't run."

Yes I can run, I can run, I can run, Tullie thought. And, flapping her arms like the wings of a big bird, she began to jump up and down to gather speed. When she was going strong, Jo Ann gave her a push and she began to hurdle across the field, toward the line that had moved in a little so she wouldn't have so far to go.

Here I come, here I come, I'm a bird and I can fly, Tullie sang to herself.

She threw herself hard at Priscilla Mayhew, but Priscilla saw her coming, screamed, and dropped her arms. On Tullie went, limping and leaping, crashing through space until she stumbled and fell into the dirt at the feet of an eighth grader who was playing outfielder for the big boys.

"Ooh," Tullie cried, and she held her skinned leg in her arms.

Miss Savage came running across the field. "Are you all right, Tullie?"

"Ooh," Tullie cried, dazed, looking at the blood trickling down her leg.

"Come with me, I'll get you to first aid." She helped Tullie up and led her across the baseball diamond toward the classrooms.

"What's the trouble?" said Miss Longer, who was on hall duty and ran the first-aid station that week.

"I'm afraid Tullie fell," Miss Savage said. "She was playing Red Rover."

"It's a rough game," Miss Longer said. "Maybe it's too rough for you, Tullie. You ought to be a little more careful." She washed off Tullie's leg, put on some Merthiolate, and a bandage. "You be more careful now, Tullie," she said. "You're not as strong as the others, you know."

Miss Savage helped Tullie back to her homeroom. Her leg was hurting and she wanted to sit down at her desk and put her white face in her arms.

"You see, Tullie," Miss Savage said, "you needn't have been afraid of Miss Longer. She likes you. She told me not to go to the principal about her watch. She said that she knows you and she is sure that it won't happen again."

That isn't true, Miss Savage, Tullie thought. I know you went to the principal, and I know he told you not to bother, that I'm too dumb to understand. I've heard him talking about me before. They all think I'm too dumb to understand. They think I'm dumb, and stupid, and crazy. They think I'm a witch because their mothers tell them my mommy is a witch.

Thinking of her mother again, Tullie began to rock back and forth in the seat, holding her hurt leg close to her. "Joy, joy," she whispered, "Joy, I've got a baby brother. When I go home today I will see my baby brother Ed. Joy to the world, my mommy will hold him up for me to see and let me play with him. Then tonight maybe my daddy will come home and we can be together, all of us together, just like a storybook family."

At the lunch hour, she sat with her back to Miss Savage and heard the other teachers talking. "I guess it's true," Mrs. Hicks was saying. "I guess there is another baby."

"Whose this time?"

"I don't know. There's a man living there now."

"What about Tullie's father?"

"No one's seen him for years."

"Is he still alive?"

"Oh yes. He has a job in the steel mills in Carson. Sends them money from time to time. When he remembers, that is."

"Do you think this will bring him back?"

"Let's hope not. He's no good. The last time he was here....
Well, Tullie was really in bad shape for a long time after that."

"What do you mean? Oh, be careful, I think she's listening."

"All right, I'll tell you later."

It wasn't true, any of it. Why did they say those things about her and her mommy? Why did Mrs. Hicks and Miss Madigan say those things about her dad? Evil things, and none of them were true. He didn't hit her, he didn't drown her dog. And her mommy was good and kind, a Disciple of Christ. Joy, joy, joy to the world, they should say. A baby boy, a brother for Tullie. Jesus has sent a little boy. Joy to the world.

"No, go ahead, she can't hear. Poor thing. She can barely see now. We have to take her in to have her eyes examined. And her teeth ... I'm really worried about her."

"The school doctor will be coming next week. He can examine her. I know that she needs special shoes."

"But who will pay for them?"

"Aren't they on welfare?"

"They can hardly make ends meet, even with that. They'll be no money for glasses or shoes or vitamins. No money for clothes."

"What will she do?"

"Come on, now, Mary. You know these kids better than that. She won't do anything. What can she do? She's poor. Every cent that that mother has will have to go for the baby now."

Miss Savage shook her head. "It's not right," she said. "It just isn't right."

"It may not be right, but that's the way it is."

"I'll help."

"You can't. They wouldn't let you. They've got pride."

"Pride? What's pride when the child is sick and needs medical attention? When she's hungry and needs proper food?"

"Stay out of it, Mary," Mr. Jenkins said. "You'll get the whole family on your head. They can manage. They have so far. You'll see. Someway or other, they'll manage."

Mary Savage left the lunchroom.

Tullie followed her in her mind's eye. Don't take on so, Miss Savage, she thought to herself. Things are all right. You see, I'm not lonely any more. I've got my lunch here, and a baby brother to play with as soon as I get home. Joy to the world!

In the afternoon, the class was tired and quiet and no one said much. Miss Savage read them a story and then they put their heads down on their desks and went to sleep, or worked quietly in their geography workbooks.

Then the bell rang, school was over, and, waving the school-bus away, Tullie limped off toward the hill that took her up the creekbed home. As she rounded the slope and could no longer see Yellowhawk behind her, she felt free and happy. Her twisted foot uncurled, her slumped shoulders straightened out. Her arms no longer flailed against the wind like huge bird wings pulling her along. She ran gracefully, happily, on fast strong feet to the dandelions and daisies that quilted the green spring meadow with brightness.

On my way home to Easter Gap,
On my way to see my pap,

> Going home to my brother Ed,
> Fast asleep in my mommy's bed.

When she came to the brown fallen tree that lay stretched across the dry creekbed, she danced over, whirling herself around and around, a zigzagging dervish pushed and pulled by the brown baron wind. She danced and leaped, full of joy, leaving the land that lay beyond behind her. Back in her own meadow, back to her own home.

"Joy to the world, joy, joy, joy to the world, Miss Savage," she sang. "Jesus looks after his own."

❧ III ❧

Edna finished wiping dry the supper dishes and stacking them in the white porcelain wall cabinet. She had just hung the dish towel in the pine tree to dry and then had come in to sit down in the leather-covered reclining chair she had given Pops last Christmas (when they had money), when she heard the screen door slam. Her hands started shaking and she tried to light a cigarette. But when she felt him standing there in the doorway her hands trembled so the match fell to the floor. Then she blushed, because he'd never seen her smoking before, and she was afraid he'd laugh at her. But he didn't.

"I've come back," he said.

"So I see."

"I...I said I've come back. I'm sorry about what happened. I really am. I'm awful sorry."

Edna didn't say a word. She just reached over and switched on the phonograph. She thought for sure that one of Pops' old records was on the turntable, but, when "String of Pearls" began to play, she closed her eyes and wanted to kick herself. He'd think she kept the phonograph just like that, with "String of Pearls" ready to go whenever he walked in the door.

"Oh, God, Edna," he said, like she knew he would.

"What's wrong?"

"That song. I remember it real well."

"I suppose you do."

He leaned against the door facing. She was glad she'd scrubbed it down that morning; it had been gray with soot from the fireplace. Now he wouldn't get that new white shirt he was wearing dirty. She'd sure hate for him to soil it in her house.

"Edna?"

"Yes?"

"Well, aren't you going to ask me to sit down? Are you going to leave me standing here in the door all night, for God's sake?"

"You didn't use to swear so much, Buddy."

"You didn't smoke, either."

So he did notice!

He slipped around the television and sat down in the rocker. He took off his straw hat and laid it on Pops' newspaper that she'd folded up just this morning. Edna was glad he didn't look at the date. The paper was two weeks old. Pops didn't buy papers too often, but he liked to see them laying around the house. He said it gave the place a look of distinction. Edna didn't think so, but there was no need to argue with him, so she always left them out. And now with him gone for a while she didn't have the heart to put them away.

"Aren't you glad to see me, Edna?"

"Sure I am."

"I'm glad to see you, too."

"It's nice of you to say that."

"I might ask you where you been."

"I could ask you the same question, Buddy."

"I guess you could." He sounded embarrassed.

"Did she quit you again?"

"I guess she did. But I never really loved her, Edna." He said it too fast—the words spilled out on top of each other and she could tell that he had been practicing his lines again.

"You loved me all the time, didn't you, Buddy?"

He began to nod.

"All the time that you was going with her."

"You're making it hard on me, Edna."

"Don't you think you made it hard on me?" She was getting mad. She hadn't intended to, she didn't want him to see how strongly she felt about him, but he made her mad. He makes me see red, she thought, no, bright orange, the color of the sun when it shines in my eyes and wakes me up in the morning because Pops can't afford to buy shutters for the windows. He makes me mad, marching in this way, without so much as a knock on the door or a "May I come in?" He makes me mad, thinking he can just barge in and I'll take him back as quick as a bluejay can sweep down and pick up a worm that lies on the sidewalk after a hard rain. Only he was the big bluejay, with his feathers all slicked down, and she was the worm, just waiting to be swooped on, and taken in by that big hard beak. Or at least that's the way he'd figured it.

Sure enough he had sidled around and was sitting on the end of her chair. The motion had tilted her back so that when he leaned up his face was just a few inches from hers.

"Come on, Edna, let's make up."

"No."

"Please, Edna," he was wheedling, just the way he'd done before. And she was beginning to weaken—she could feel it. She knew that her arms were wanting to reach up and slip around his neck. She knew her lips were wanting to be pressed against his.

She twisted around and changed the record. She put on one of Pops' favorites, an old ballad. She figured that would cool him off.

He pulled back, surprised.

Not as easy as you thought, is it? she wanted to say to him. But she couldn't. To save her life, she couldn't say those words. She couldn't bring herself to hurt him, the way he'd hurt her.

"How's Pops?" he asked finally.

"He's doing better."

"The doctors treat him well?"

"As good as any doctors will treat a poor man."

"How long do you think it's going to take this..."

"This time? I don't know." She had started to cry. She didn't want him to see her crying but she couldn't help it. She squinted hard to keep back the tears, but it didn't do any good. She always got upset when she thought about Pops because, deep down in her heart, she didn't think a man could ever be cured of the liquor habit.

He saw the tears and moved toward her and she felt herself being tilted back again. It was going to be harder to say no this time.

"Edna, come on, let's make up. Maybe I can help out."

"You could of helped out before," she blurted out. "But not

now. It was you who caused Pops' sickness this time. You've got that on your conscience, and I'm not going to clear it by taking you back."

He was startled. "I . . . I don't know what you mean."

"Oh, you don't, don't you?" she gulped. "Pops thought you were going to marry me . . . like we told him. He was real happy —the happiest he's been since Mom died. He thought he could die happy, he told me, seeing me out of—here—and getting settled down in a nice clean little house with an educated man. He really believed that, Buddy. He said, 'Buddy's going to take care of my little girl for me.' "

Buddy looked so white that she stopped. She really couldn't bear hurting him so, by giving him all the blame.

"Well, he might have felt the tremble coming on when he said it. He might have known then that he couldn't be taking care of me much longer. And he knew that it would be hard for me to make a living myself—being as how I'm not so well ed-ucated, you know."

"Go on."

"What more is there to tell? You went back to her. I didn't tell Pops you'd left again. I just sort of pretended that you'd gone out of town on business. But he saw you. He saw you riding around with her—he said you were driving her car down past Yellowhawk where everybody could see you all and say, 'Why, isn't that Buddy Bradford with Ray Mitchell's girl?' He said when he stopped in the store that evening, he saw all the men laughing and nudging each other behind their newspapers. He knew then that you'd not be back. He started going back to the bar soon after."

"Oh, God," Buddy said in a voice as low as a worn out preacher who's just said his last amen on Sunday evening. "Oh, God."

There wasn't a sound in the house, only the steady tick tock of the cuckoo. A painted cuckoo clock, at that, not a real one with a music box, like Buddy's aunt had in her sitting room.

"Is . . . is there anything I could do for him? Maybe some money?"

"Oh, no," she said, almost choking on the words, he had stung her so. "We don't want your money, Buddy. I can make out fine, thank you."

"How?"

"There's ways," she said darkly.

"Don't talk that way, Edna." He reached over and started shaking her hard. He's shaking me harder than he's ever held me, she thought. His face was getting all pink, and that surprised her. She'd always been told that black-haired people never really blush, but Buddy came as close to it then as she'd ever seen one do. She just sat there, letting him shake her until her teeth rattled and watching his face lose its pink flush and go white again. Finally he got tired of shaking her and sat back down.

"You want to get married now?"

"Why?" she asked, holding her breath.

"Well... it might help Pops."

So that was it.

"And ... and I do love you, Edna."

"No, you don't, Buddy. You want me, but you don't love me. And you couldn't stay away from rich people because you don't feel strongly enough for me. It would just be a mess. A bigger mess than it is now."

"If that's the way you feel, Edna." He sounded relieved. "But I'll ask you one more time. Do you want to marry me? Right now. No postponement. We'll go and do it now."

"No, Buddy."

His face really fell with her second refusal. He'd been pretty sure that the fish would bite this time.

"Thank you, but no." It sounded pretty final, as if someone else were saying it. Not me, she thought. I'm not grand enough to be saying no to Buddy Bradford.

But she knew that she had done it when she saw him reach for his hat and push it down on his head. Then he walked across the floor and opened the screen door.

"Edna?"

"Good-by, Buddy."

The door closed and after a minute or two she couldn't hear his footsteps any more. She just sat there, half tilted back in the chair, feeling poor and stupid and lonely. Pops was in the hospital, Buddy was gone for good, and she was left alone with the bitter taste of her pride. All she could think about was that life wasn't fair to girls like her. She was only seventeen but nobody would want her because she'd been Buddy Bradford's girl and everybody knew that Buddy was mean and good looking and got what he wanted from the girls. She put "String of Pearls" back on the phonograph and started to cry. "I wish I'd said yes," she said out loud. "I wish I'd said yes."

She almost expected to hear the door open and see Buddy step back inside. After all, hadn't she really thought he had been waiting around outside for her to change her mind? After all, didn't he know her well enough to know she would change her mind because she'd do anything she could for Pops? She'd even swallow her pride and take a man on the rebound. She began to smile, as she sat there listening for the door to open and Buddy to walk back in and sweep her up into his arms. She leaned her head over on her shoulder and smiled, thinking about herself in a new white dress, carrying a bouquet of flowers and smiling at everyone who had come to the church to see her get married to Buddy Bradford. "She got him back," they'd say. "She lost him once, but she got him back." And she sat there a long time before she realized that she was alone again and Buddy would not be coming back.

❧ IV ❧

The sickly sweet smell of apple syrup coming to the boil filled her nostrils, choking her out of her cool green apple dreams and bringing her full awake, gagging, on the pillow.

"Glenda," Mom called. "Glenda, get down here and help me with the sugar."

"Coming, Mom."

The girl pulled herself up and tugged at her pajamas, dropping them to the floor and reaching for the skirt and blouse draped across the foot of the bed.

"Pray, Glenda," Mom called. "Don't forget to pray."

"Aren't you in a hurry, Mom?"

"Pray with your thoughts."

"I'll pray," Glenda promised. "Come home, Jim," she said with her tongue tucked back as far as she could push it, to keep the gurgle of sickness from washing up her throat. "Come home, Jim. Today."

Outside, the blackness was lifting and a jagged smile of orange sun streaked the grass-whiskered cheek of ridge and cabin perched against a grim fence of scrawny trees. Day came, a late August morning, with those hot winds that wiggle their way to the roots of a girl's long brown hair, tickling and stinging as they cool away the sweat of fear and sickness.

Down the stairs, to the kitchen, where Mom was standing at the stove, stirring the blue-speckled pan that was gurgling viciously beneath each stroke of the wooden spoon.

"You take it," Mom said with a nod. "I'll measure the sugar."

Not looking into the pan, Glenda stirred, feeling her head grow dizzy as she traced the hot blue metal walls, grinding away at the lumps, holding down the syrup that threatened to rise up and bubble over the pan, over the stove, over her skirt and sandaled feet, over the scrubbed linoleum floor, spreading its sweetness across the ridge and down the hollow, pushing down flowers, trapping sycamore balls, tracking the footprints of wind that have covered the steps of wily Jim, who came and loved and left.

"Maybe I should let it go," she thought. "Maybe I should let it rise and ribbon loose, then I could run dancing, sticky footed, through it."

"What are you waiting for?" Mom asked. "That sugar's going to harden."

She stirred, patting the wooden spoon against the pan bottom, pounding out the knots, whetting the sugar powder that sifts down in a hard mass, then cowers lumpishly under the flow of apple syrup, resisting its amalgamation.

"You look peaked," Mom said. "Didn't you get to sleep last night?"

"Yes. But I was awake awhile."

"Studying hard?"

"Yes." Glenda pulled herself up straight and tried to look at Mom directly.

Mom handed her a cup of coffee.

"School's too hard for girls who have to help out at home," she said. "You shouldn't be going."

"Oh, but Mom..."

"No. You shouldn't. I don't know why I let you talk me into it again this year."

"But it's my last year," Glenda cried. "This is the eighth grade. After this, I'll be through..."

"Then you'll start begging to go to high school," Mom said, pulling down her upper lip.

"No, I won't."

"I know you. A sixteen-year-old girl who's not ashamed to sit in the eighth grade with kids two and three years younger than her won't be ashamed to start in high school three years later."

"I won't ask to go," Glenda promised. "If you'll just let me finish up."

"I don't like the school," Mom said.

"Yellowhawk's a fine school, a new school, and it's clean. There's good books there, and a big playground."

"Playground! What do you need a playground for? And what good have you got out of books? All you need's your Bible, and I don't see you reading much of that."

"Every night, Mom. And every morning, when I can."

Suddenly, her eyes meeting the six o'clock sun that flooded through the kitchen window, Mom saw God's universe seething with life on Dummit Ridge. She saw the sun fireball through blue-gray sky, lighting His path, she saw the trees bow down their leaves beneath a rod of wind, she heard wakening birds chorus out hymns in His praise. Forgetting the jelly, forgetting her daughter, her mind fortified by the mystery of the morning, her eyes dropped in anguish to her flattened breasts, her long-sleeved arms, her slack belly.

Seeing her mom caught up in the trance, Glenda pulled the pan from the stove and lowered the fire. Then, creeping away to the wash pan beneath the stairs, she swabbed off her sweating face, and rinsed her arms and feet and legs. Her books were stacked neatly by the door, ready in case she must slip them out. Her long fingers gently raised and lowered the latch, and her heel caught the screen door in its slam.

At last, she was gone.

But not only she is gone.

Where is Jim Hamilton?

Morning, thick and succulent as a frog's throat bellowing through nippy air, turned its cry to her. Where is Jim Hamilton? The sun, now dripping and oozing out of its riveted cloud silt, burned through her sun-browned cheeks. It left a fresh brand, a sweating mark of shame. She stopped at the creek to wash away the fiery blush. In the creek waters, there are two faces. Hers and the face of another girl, a girl she does not know, a woman staring at her in dumb, frightened silence, too afraid to speak, too afraid to remain silent. Where is Jim Hamilton? The lips of the other move uncertainly. Glenda stared at them, unable to reply. With knobby fingers, she strokes the cheeks, the neck, the aching sides of the stranger who is following her. "What can I do for you?" she asks.

"Find me Jim Hamilton," the young woman replies, tears in her brown shadow eyes.

"I am trying," Glenda assures her, reaching out, and up, to wipe away the tears.

"Find him quickly."

"I am trying."

"Soon it will be too late."

Crouched in the moss, her heels haunched on soft green leaves, Glenda pushed her hands into the mounded clay at the creek bank's edge. The clay was sticky, crumbly, stinking. It decayed in her hand, leaving only a mass of silt.

"Thus is man," boomed a voice from behind. "Thus is man, all clay, until the breath of God blown upon him masticates his essence with the glory of the soul, the glory of Christ, and gives him being."

Glenda turned, trembling.

"Come to me, my child, and be forgiven."

Crouching had strained her muscles, and she toppled from her effort to rise, catching her toe on a sharp rock.

"You are heavy from your burden," said the man, his red beard tufty and silken in the echo he threw at her feet.

"Come to me, Glenda Robards, I am life and I shall save you and forgive you for the sin you have committed."

Terror spreading across her face, terror wrinkling her lips into a frown of disbelief and denial, Glenda reached for her books, ready to run.

"Wait," called the man, holding out his hand. "Wait in the name of the Lord and His messenger, Jim Hamilton."

She stopped.

"Yes, I have come to you, Glenda," he said. "I have come to speak to you of your sin, and of his."

"I have done no sin."

"Pride, my daughter, is a wicked and evil thing. Pride is far more to be feared than sin itself, for we who do not know God are ignorant in our sin—it is our pride that denies that we have done wrong, when we are told our wrongs, and shown the way, and given the opportunity to repent and live and walk in the ways of our lord God."

"No," said the young woman who stared up at Glenda from the blue water. "No, be careful."

"I have come from the church, to tell you of Jim Hamilton, who came crying to my altars, crying out his sin, and yours, and begging me to come to you, to forgive you and bring you back to the paths of righteousness."

"I have done no sin."

"Be careful, my daughter! The child within you will some day rise up and stone you himself! He will cast each rock, and with each rock the cry, 'This is my mother, and I am her bastard son! She would not admit her wrong, and walk in the ways of God—but I shall follow in the footsteps of my father, and leave her to her own perdition!' "

"Where is Jim Hamilton?" Glenda asked.

"He is a suppliant in my chapel. I have given him refuge, and instruction in the ways of the Lord. He will be my follower, my apostle. He will walk the paths of Dummit Ridge and the streets of the town, telling all that God is God and man is man and the two must meet before it is too late."

"What do you want of me?"

"Come with me. I shall protect you from the vicious years that lie ahead, when you and your fatherless child confront the multitudes and are spit upon."

"The child is not fatherless."

"I shall forgive you of your sin, and show you the way to divine forgiveness."

"I have done no sin."

"No sin?" The man bellowed in a voice as red as his beard. "No sin? You have lain with a man outside the bonds of marriage. You have conceived his child and you will bear a bastard son sired of the devil himself since you had no husband."

Frightened, Glenda looked down at the bare, corn-ridden feet of the preacher. His toes, squishing in and out of the mound of clay he had stepped on, left their imprints in its sticky surface.

"Come with me, and I will make you a follower. I will show you to the multitudes, and tell them of your sin. I will marry you to Jim Hamilton in the name of the Lord, but you will not live with him again! You will do eternal penitence by your denial, thus showing all our followers that God is good, that God is divine, that God forgives those who have sinned against Him, but then sought out His charity. And of your child, I shall make of him a priest, a pure man whose chastity will absolve his mother's lack of it."

Sick in her stomach from the light in the bearded man's brown eyes and the harsh sound of his voice, Glenda turned her head away. The creek showed her the stranger and at his feet the young woman who looked beseechingly into his wild brown eyes.

"I know now," she whispered to the water image. "I know where Jim Hamilton has gone."

She brought up her books, wiping off the grit that had stuck to them. She stepped back, and saw that the young woman in the water was fading into ripples, as the preacher threw rocks into the water, crying out that life is like the ripples of a rock, riding out toward the unknown, to be swooped up by the hands of God and nestled in His bosom.

From the foot of the ridge, she heard the screech of brakes as the schoolbus stopped to pick up the children who had gathered there at the covered bridge to ride to Yellowhawk.

"Too late," she realized. "Too late for the bus today."

The preacher, too, heard the bus and the sound of children laughing and scrambling on board.

"The sounds of progress," he mumbled, shaking his head. "They go too far now. They forget their Maker, in their hurry to learn more, to do more, to see more of this world's riches. I thank God for men like Jim Hamilton, who see their ruin in time, men who are not too proud to ask for another chance, another start in life, men who are..."

"Cowards," Glenda cried. She remembered her mother, praying fanatically at the kitchen window while the jelly boiled and burnt in the tin pan that Glenda would have to scrub. Turning, slipping on slick leaves, she stretched out one lean foot to begin to run down the ridge path toward the stile that mounted the fence and led down the road to the covered bridge.

But the preacher's strong hand snapped up her wrist and held it in a lockfast grip.

"No, Glenda Robards. You don't escape me that easily. I'll not have you running for help. You're caught."

Glenda trembled and fought back the tears of fright and the sobbing rhythm rising in her throat.

"I'll not have you running away, down there, to the outside world, to shame yourself and my son—"

Cold with the slick sweat of fear, Glenda stared at the ruddy-faced man who grinned down upon her from his stocky six feet.

"I'll not have you shame my son," he repeated. "We'll not be the laughingstock of Yellowhawk."

"But, I..."

"And my son will take no ridge-born witch as wife."

"Where are you taking me?"

"To your mother," the Reverend Hamilton told her. "But it's you who are taking me there. To tell her of your conversion. To gather up your things. And to follow me, as a penitent, to the church in the valley."

It was as if the sugar syrup had risen and bubbled over the old scorched pan, over the stove, over the scrubbed-linoleum floor, spreading its sweetness across the ridge, tracking her, trapping her, holding her fast to the ridge and the way of life she had tried to break away from.

V

When cousin Vianella got sick and Bob Brady sent for Loretta's Pa to fetch him home, Pa shook his head and said, "It's his head or his friends."

Loretta figured it was his head, because Vi was the shy sort and never did take much to town folks; but Pa held that that was the very reason of his pains—that he was lonesome, now that his pa and mom were gone, and he'd been boarded out to Bob Brady to clerk all day in that crumbly store, when he wasn't put to splittin' kindling and toting wash water for Mrs. Brady.

So, on Monday morning, when Pa took the old car and went for Vianella, Loretta begged to go along, but no, he said, she'd only cry for rock candy and hair ribbons, and he had neither the money to buy nor the heart to refuse.

So she pouted until she saw Pa meant what he'd said. Then she fixed up a bed for Vi in the back room, just a cot spread with a quilt his ma had made, but then, men never did know the difference; and put on a hambone and bay leaf to start some vegetable soup. When Vi's parents passed, all poor Vi could keep down for weeks was vegetable soup. He said it sort of slicked down his stomach before he knew what had hit him. Loretta didn't take kindly to his compliments, but Pa said it was the best he could do.

It was a warm April afternoon when Pa puttered up the road in the car. Loretta ran to the porch as soon as she heard the motor, and strained her eyes for sight of them. She half expected to see poor Vi stretched out in the back seat, covered with blankets to keep down the chills, and maybe with Mrs. Brady's sulfur medicine spread over his poor pimply forehead.

But there he sat, in the front seat beside Pa, large as life, his shaggy hair blowing in the breeze, his chin sticky from the rock candy he was chewing. He and Pa were grinning and chattering away. When the old car heaved to a stop, Vi slung his bags out of the back, and loped up the path.

"Hiya, Loretta," he grinned.

"Hullo, Vianella."

His huge hand tumbled playfully over her head. She stepped back.

"What's the matter? My favorite cousin—and a girl at that—gone timid as a rabbit?"

"No," she said slowly.

"Well?"

"I'm just...surprised...Vi."

"How come?" He dropped his bags with a thud.

"I thought...Pa said...I mean..."

"Oh, Brady had me pictured as halfway to glory, eh? Now isn't that just like him? That featherhead! You know, Loretta, I think his head is stuffed plum full of those feathers he sleeps on. Maybe Miz Brady plumps him up in the morning, too!"

"Here you go, girl," Pa said, with a big happy smile. He shoved a white sack into her hands.

"What's this? Candy, Pa?"

"What's left of it. Your cousin had a hunger fit on the way home..."

Loretta gave Vi a look that would have frozen a streak of sunlight. Then she went in the house and slammed the screen as hard as she could.

Vi was hot on her heels.

"Dear Loretta," he said. "Dear Cousin Loretta—don't feel hard toward me. I got you something to make up for it."

"I don't want it. What is it?"

"A handful of Mr. Brady's best taffeta ribbons!"

"I don't want them."

"All shades of green," he went on. "I picked them out, especially for you, to match your eyes. Why, I'll bet when you wear them on Sunday, you'll have all the fellers at the First Methodist so fixed on you, the preacher couldn't get to them for all his threats of hellfire and green damnation!"

"Shut up, Vi!" Loretta hollered. "Shut up and leave me alone.

I don't want any part of your old ribbons. You probably snitched them from Mrs. Brady's sewing basket. And I don't want any part of you—lying the way you did, scaring the wits out of Pa and me. Why there's nothing wrong with you! You're just lazy! Too much work for you at the store. You figured you'd come back here, where I'd cook and wash for you, and Pa'd take care of you. I know you, Vianella Parsons! And I won't do it! Pa and I get along fine, and we don't need you around."

"Loretta," Pa said sternly. "Go to your room."

"I will," she said. "I'll go to my room, and I won't come out. Ever."

Pa took a step forward and she ran. She ran up the stairs and hid behind the railing. Then she saw Vi turn to Pa. His mouth was quivering.

"I'm sorry, Uncle Beecher," he said. "Don't take it out on Loretta. I teased her—I shouldn't have. She's just a kid."

"I'm not," Loretta cried out from behind the banister, forgetting she was supposed to be in her room. "I'm no kid, Vi! I'm as grown-up as you! I'm twelve and you're only eighteen! Don't you call me a kid!"

"Get in your room!" Pa shouted. "And don't slam the door!"

She went in and lay down on the bed. She put her head on Mom's crocheted pillow and cried. Then she must have fallen asleep, for the next thing she knew, Pa was sitting there beside her.

"Loretta," he said, shaking her, "Loretta, wake up."

She opened her eyes and looked up at him. Then she remembered what had happened, and started to cry again. She and Pa never argued, and he scarcely ever had to raise his voice to her.

"Loretta, I'm going to tell you something," he said softly. "And I want you to listen. Don't ask me any questions. I can't answer them—partly because I don't know all the answers. But I trust you, and I want you to trust me."

Loretta nodded. She understood Pa when he talked to her this way.

"Loretta, Vianella's going to be staying with us for a while. Now I don't know how long. But he's going to make his home with us, and I want you to treat him right, like he was your own brother. Don't fly off the handle at him. What's happened to him, I don't know. But right now he needs a family, more than ever. He's only eighteen, and he's alone in the world except for us. We're going to be his family. I'm going to be his pa, and you, his sister. Understand?"

"Yes, Pa."

"And you'll treat him right?"

"Yes. But, Pa ..."

"Remember, Loretta, no questions."

"All right, Pa."

"Come on downstairs, now."

Loretta got up and combed her hair. On the dresser were Vi's ribbons. She fastened them in her pigtails, and pressed out her skirt where it had wrinkled. Then she went down to the kitchen.

Vi was sitting at the table, looking out the window.

"Did you find your room, Vi?"

"Yes."

"I fixed it up some this morning."

"Thanks, Loretta."

"You're gettin' hungry?"

"A little."

"I put some soup on this morning."

He smiled. "That'll be fine."

They didn't say a word about what had happened earlier. Loretta didn't ask Vi any questions, and he didn't talk on his own accord.

Things went on that way for three months. Vi stayed at the house and helped Pa. Loretta was surprised to see that boy work so hard. He did everything he could for Pa. He was up at daylight, and out in the field until dusk. He never complained; he never asked for a cent of spending money for Saturday nights. He never asked leave to go to town, either. He seemed content right there, with them, on the farm.

On the first Sunday Vi was there, Loretta asked Pa if they'd be bringing anyone for dinner. Sometimes they asked old Mrs. Belfry to come home with them after church and spend the afternoon.

Mrs. Belfry was in her seventies, and she kept up on all the town gossip. She'd talk a blue streak from the time she got in the car until they took her home at milking time. She had told Loretta all about the barber's boy and the postman's daughter, who were going to run away and get married, but the barber kept watching them, and about the hats in Miss Sally's windows, and the new dress material—silk and satin and organdy—she kept ordering from Philadelphia. That Mrs. Belfry was smart! She could remember the cut of a dress down to the way the lace was put on the sleeves. Sometimes she'd sketch out a pattern for Loretta, and help her arrange her lengths of dimity cotton for cutting.

Mrs. Belfry had a good heart. She gave Loretta quilt pieces, and embroidery floss, and taught her to match buttons for mending Pa's shirts. Loretta liked Mrs. Belfry.

"No, Loretta," Pa said slowly. "We're not going to church this morning."

Loretta looked up, surprised. Just then Vi came in the door. "But, Pa, I ..."

"So, if you want to fry your chicken now, I'll have Vi to pluck it for you."

"All right," Loretta said, guessing Pa didn't want Vi to know what they'd been saying.

"Will you, Vi?"

"Sure thing," he grinned.

So, Vi stayed on, and they kept to themselves. Loretta didn't even ask to play with the Carter children. She had the feeling that Pa didn't want her to, or he'd have mentioned it. But she wasn't lonely. In fact, she was happier than she'd ever been since Mom died. Pa wrote for some books for her, and Vi helped her on the hard words. Vi even knew a little Latin—his mom had been a teacher—and he started teaching his cousin in the evenings. He said she'd never get much chance to learn another language around here. Loretta was surprised to see how smart Vi was. Once she saw him reading a book on philosophy. She asked him where he got it, and he said it had belonged to his mom.

But Vi wasn't all lessons. He made her dolls from cornshucks, dolls with yarn hair and button eyes and pokeberry ink mouths and eyelashes. When she dressed the dolls, Vi even helped her choose the scraps of material for their dresses.

He spent one entire Sunday afternoon hammering and sawing in the smokehouse. When he came in for supper, he had a tiny rocking chair and table for Loretta's dolls. He said he'd try to make her a little bed, too, if she thought she could manage a canopy for it. Loretta remembered then that Vi's mom had slept in a bed with a canopy, so she said she'd try her best. She found some little wires, and Vi helped her stretch a piece of white cotton across them. Then they dug up some scraps of lace from old pillowcases, and trimmed the edges. When Vi finished the bed, they fastened the canopy on top, and put one of the small dolls in. Then Loretta brought out her surprise—she had cut another piece of white cotton for a spread, and embroidered a pink flower on it. Vi was pleased.

When Pa came in, he looked at them and smiled. Then he picked up the tiny bed and held it in his big hands. "It's a beauty, Vi," he said. "Did you do it?"

Vi just grinned.

"No, I couldn't have done better," Pa said. "Matter of fact, Vi, I don't think a carpenter could beat this. Loretta, why don't you leave it downstairs, where we all can see it?"

"All right," she said. "But can I take it up at night?"

"Sure," Pa laughed.

So they set the bed and the table and chair in the front room on the highboy. Loretta put some acorns on the tiny table for dishes, and fringed a little cloth and napkins.

Early the morning after Vi had finished the bed, Loretta was getting ready to fry eggs when she heard a car drive up in front of the house. A horn sounded. That horn frightened her—she dropped the egg she had just cracked. People around there never blew their horns, they hollered.

She thought a minute, then went to the front door.

"Hello," she said.

A tall man was sitting in the front seat, one hand on the steering wheel, and one on the car door. Two other men were with him. One of them had a rifle.

"Hello," the man at the wheel said.

"Does Vianella Parsons live here?" the man with the rifle shouted. He had a mean tone to his voice. Loretta didn't answer him.

"I'll call my Pa," she said.

"Yes, we want to see him, too," the third man said.

But Pa was already behind her. "Go to your room, Loretta," he said. "Quick!"

"Pa..."

"You heard me."

She turned toward the stairs. She saw Vi standing by the railing. He had a rifle in his hand. She'd never seen Vi like this—he looked tall and thin, and scared. His lip was trembling, and his shaggy hair kept falling in his eyes.

"What is it, Vi?" she whispered. "What's wrong?"

"Nothing, Loretta," he said. His voice quivered. "Go on in your room, like your pa tol' you. Don't come out until he calls you."

Then Vi started slowly down the stairs.

Inside her room, Loretta could hear voices—loud, angry voices. She heard the man with the ugly voice swearing, and she heard Pa answer him. Her pa had never sounded this way—not even when he scolded her. Now his voice was as low and hard and mean as the voice of the man in the car.

Finally one of the men shouted at the top of his lungs, "We know he's there, Beecher! We know it! And we won't leave without him! Didn't you understand what I said? I said I'm the sheriff of this county, and I've come for Vianella Parsons. He's under arrest. Now I didn't come out here to pay a friendly call, I came to..." His voice dwindled away as the front door slammed.

They were out there for a long time. Loretta lay on Mom's crocheted pillow, and waited for Pa and Vi to come back.

When the door opened, Pa was by himself. He was holding Vi's rifle.

"What happened, Pa?" Loretta asked. "What happened?"

Pa sat down on the bed beside her. He laid the rifle on the floor.

"Vi's gone," he said. He sounded tired and old.

"Gone, Pa? Gone where?"

Pa sat for a long time without saying a word. Then, he said, "Loretta, when Vi came to stay with us, I asked you to trust me—not to question me, or question Vi. I told you there were a lot of things I didn't know—and a lot of answers I couldn't give you. I knew Vi was in trouble. And I knew it was bad trouble. But I had the feeling Vi wasn't at fault—that boy is the son of my brother. He wouldn't have come back to us if he'd done wrong.

"I never asked him what it was that had happened. He never told me. But there was talk of a shooting—talk that Vi had shot a man. The man wasn't a good man—he insulted Vi, and he talked bad about Vi's pa. He needled the boy, kept coming back to Brady's store, and talking; he said some pretty ugly things about Tom Parsons and his wife. Finally, Vi lost his temper and shot the man. That's when Brady sent me word that Vi was sick—he wanted him got out of town. Well, the man Vi shot died this morning."

"Where's Vi?" Loretta cried. "I don't care what happened to that man, or why Vi shot him! Where's Vi? Where've they taken him?"

"He has to stand trial," Pa said. Then he left the room.

The weeks that followed were long ones. Pa went to town each morning. They didn't talk much about what had happened when he came home, and the only real news Loretta had of Vi was through Mrs. Belfry. She said it looked pretty bad. She said Pa had hired a good lawyer, and the boy was young and had been insulted—that was in his favor. But she said it looked bad.

Loretta mooned around the house, playing with her dolls and the bed and table and chairs Vi had made her. Finally she put them away—she couldn't look at them without crying.

One evening when Pa came back, he said he wouldn't need to be going to town any more. He said it was all over.

"Pa," Loretta said, "Pa, what's happened? It's been four weeks now.... What's happened to Vi?"

Pa lifted her up on his lap, like he used to do when she was a little girl, and put his big arms around her.

"Loretta, there's some things we never will be able to understand," he said. "Things we just have to accept and learn to live with." He looked away.

"What are they going to do with Vi?" she whispered.

"Honey, they hanged him this morning."

She got up slowly, she couldn't look at Pa. She stood by the door for a long time, remembering the April morning Pa and Vi had driven up in the old car—Vi, tall and lanky and lonely, was laughing and teasing her with a handful of green ribbons.

Then she gathered up the cornshuck dolls, the canopied bed, the rocking chair, the little table with a fringed cloth and acorn dishes. She took them up to her room, and put them on the dresser. She set one of the dolls on Mom's pillow. She packed away Vi's clothes, and put his books in her room, by the window. She spread the quilt Vi's mom had made over her bed.

Then she went downstairs to cook supper.

❧ VI ❧

When she was a young girl living on the farm, Jenny Jones spent her evenings looking at the moon and the hills that were always white, summer and winter, in the eastern Kentucky moonlight. Her bedroom window opened onto the flat of the ridge and overlooked the Sandy River far below and far away. Beyond the Sandy, the hills were black with trees and shadows. When she was a child, Jenny was afraid of Ohio and the darkness of a land that did not show its face to moonlight.

Growing up on the farm and in the First Methodist Church, her mother in the choir and her daddy a deacon, Jenny learned not to be afraid of God's night or His day, of the workings of His hand and the wonders of His mind. She loved the wild flowers that grew in the fields alongside the tomatoes and beans and corn. She loved the hills and the trees, the day when man worked and prayed, and the night when it was time to pray and sleep. When Jenny went to church, she always listened to the preacher's sermon because Reverend Jack's eyes were wild and they went all over the congregation, fastening first on this face and then on that one and she was terrified that he would catch her not listening and call her down the way he had once called down Elizabeth Sparks who used to sit and dream of Billy Hicks.

So Jenny loved life and the day and tried hard not to be afraid of the dark, God's dark. She was a smart girl, her mother said, and her daddy said that she was the brightest one of all the Joneses. They knew that if she lived right and did right, if she studied and learned, if she was a good girl and obeyed her parents and prayed to God, she would grow up to be a fine woman, the kind of woman who would be right in the eyes of Man and God.

Jenny went to school and studied and learned and was a good

girl. She made her parents proud of her. When they took her to town on Saturdays, the people would say, "There goes Jenny Jones. Isn't she a pretty child!" And as she grew up, the old people would still say, "There goes Jenny. Isn't she a good girl!" When she was ready to go away to college they said, "You're going to be somebody, Jenny. You're going to make us proud of you. Someday you'll make us all proud of you. You're going to put this town on the map."

Jenny went away to Tennessee on the night train. Her daddy found her a seat in a coach where no one was sitting, told her to be a good girl and remember the way she was raised, and then went home. Jenny sat alone in the coach, wanting a drink of water but afraid to walk the way to the fountain. For the first time since she had grown up, she was afraid of the dark.

She kept her hand on her pocketbook all the way to Knoxville, and her suitcase at her feet. She was afraid to go to sleep, not knowing what might happen to her if somebody came walking through her coach and saw her sitting there alone, asleep, with her pocketbook on the seat by her. When she got hungry, she ate the meal her mother had packed for her in a paper bag. And she didn't get up from her seat until daylight came and she had to go and find the bathroom.

The University of Tennessee was big and there was no special place for good girls with the right kind of upbringing to go and be by themselves. Jenny found her way to the scholarship office, the registration lines, the cafeteria, the dormitory. She found her way to classes and back to the library, the cafeteria and the dormitory. She found her way to church on Sundays, the cafeteria, the library, and back to church again on Sunday evenings. She liked her roommate, who called her hokey behind her back, but they didn't have much to say to each other, and Gayle Sowards swore she wouldn't have anything to do with her when she saw that Jenny didn't have any clothes she wanted to borrow.

"That Jenny," she would say to the other girls. "She's really something. Hokey, you know. Nothing but work, you know."

Jenny was a little bit afraid of Gayle who kept a crucifix by her bed and must have been Catholic. Jenny had never known any Catholics before, but she had heard about them, and she didn't know how she should behave around them. So she stayed quiet and let Gayle do most of the talking, when there was anything to say.

Little by little, the first year went by and Jenny came home with thirty hours of A commendations from the Dean, and her scholarship renewed for next year. Her daddy had it put in the newspaper, and Jenny blushed when she was back in town on Saturdays and people would stop her on the street to say, "Well, Miss Jenny Jones, didn't I tell you that you were going to do something? Didn't I tell you that you were going to be somebody? I'll bet you get this town on the map yet."

She went back to Knoxville, nineteen years old and a sophomore at the University. She wasn't so afraid this time, only homesick. She knew her way around, she could stand aside and smile at the new freshmen running around like a bunch of chickens with their heads cut off to find the registration lines, the scholarship office, the classrooms, and the cafeteria.

"Just look at them all," Gayle Sowards said, when she met Jenny standing outside the Dean of Women's office, waiting to see the list and find out what dormitory she was in. "Aren't they a hokey-looking outfit?"

And Gayle smiled at Jenny because she had just been in to see Dean Briarley, and the Dean had told her that she and Jenny were going to be roommates again because the Dean felt that Gayle was doing so much for Jenny Jones.

"Just what do you think of that?" Gayle had said to her friends. "Did you ever think of me as some small-town kid's baby sitter? Do I look the part? That hokey girl. Another year of her."

But the more she thought about it, the more she liked the idea. "Me," Gayle thought. "They've asked old C+ me to do something for old A+ Jenny. Maybe I ought to try to do something for her! Maybe I ought to try to loosen her up a little, get her out of the library, let her see what life at college is all about." But whenever she looked at Jenny, her heart sank. Jenny would never loosen up. She was all wound up inside herself, books in arm, headed for the library, the classroom, the cafeteria, the dormitory, and church.

"What does life mean to you?" Gayle wanted to ask as she

watched Jenny getting ready for bed each night with the same sure slow movements that Gayle had memorized last year. "What do you think it's all about? Or do you ever think about it?"

But at least Gayle didn't mind sleeping with the light on. "Everybody's got his funny side," she told her friends. "And old Jenny is afraid of the dark." It wasn't that she was really afraid of the dark, though. It was just that, coming back to Tennessee for the second year, it was so much lonelier. All the newness was gone. All the excitement which had terrified her at first and then exhilarated her, had been replaced by the calm of familiar things. Jenny stood looking at her school calendar, realizing that it would be a long year before she would once again be home for the summer. A long year of life inside buildings, surrounded by books and papers and people who would never become a part of her.

And so, when one Saturday night the girl who was double dating with Gayle and her steady boy friend Frank Harris didn't show up, Jenny said Yes, she would go along. It was her second year in college and she still hadn't accepted a date. She didn't know what to wear, she didn't know what to do, or what to expect she would have to do. Gayle picked out her clothes, got her dressed, and dragged her down the stairs to where the boys were waiting in the dormitory reception room.

It was love at first sight for Jenny. Tri South was the best-looking boy she had ever seen. He was tall, he had short blond hair and beautiful brown eyes. He stood up when Gayle introduced them, and put his hand under her elbow to lead her out to the car.

Frank drove with Gayle sitting as close to him as she could get. Jenny sat in the back with Tri, wondering what she should say or what he was going to say to her. Tri was quiet at first, looking at Jenny out of the corner of his eye. He asked her where she was from, and she told him. Then she asked him where he was from, and he told her. Up in the front seat, Gayle was giggling. Jenny began to turn red and shrink toward the door of the car. Here she was, out on her first college date, and she didn't know what to do. She was humiliated; the only thing she could think of was getting out of the car and back to the safety of her dormitory and the comfort of her books. "I didn't know I'm this awful," she thought. "Why, no wonder they laugh at me. I'm from another world. I'm not even living in the twentieth century."

They reached the movie and Frank parked the car. When they got out, Jenny said to Tri, "I'm sorry but I'm going home. No, I can catch a bus. There's one that goes back to the campus."

"What's wrong?" he said. "Are you sick?"

"No," Jenny said, as she was starting to cry. "I'm just all wrong. I didn't realize it until tonight, but I'm all wrong."

"Honey, if I did something..."

"No," Jenny sobbed, "that's just it. You're perfect. But I'm... I'm all wrong."

Tri stood staring at her, his head cocked at one side. She was almost pretty, he thought. A little too tall, and a funny head that didn't seem to know which way to turn, but she was almost pretty.

"Look, gang," he said to Gayle and Frank. "You go on. We're going to take a little walk. See you later."

"But..." Gayle was signaling him with her eyes. That's not Kathy, she was saying; that's Jenny. You don't know what you're getting in for."

"See you folks," Tri said, as he marched Jenny off down the street.

They went into a restaurant and Tri ordered coffee. Then he asked Jenny what was wrong, and put his arm around her to stop her shaking. Jenny sobbed into her napkin and said that she had never realized how awful she was, how small town, how naive, how awful. "I'm hokey," she said. "I know I am. I'm hokey."

Tri laughed and ran his fingers through his short blond hair. Then he squeezed her arm. "Honey," he said. "That word's out. Nobody uses it any more."

"But Gayle does," Jenny sobbed, ashamed to be sitting here in this greasy spoon on her first college date sobbing to the boy who'd brought her along as a favor because his own date hadn't shown.

"Gayle Sowards doesn't know half what she thinks she does," Tri said. "And don't let me catch you listening to her any more. Unless you want a good laugh."

It made Jenny smile to think of Gayle being run down by Tri. It made her smile to think that she was being looked after by Tri.

"You're all right," Tri said, putting his arm around her a little tighter. "You really are. You know, you're the first real girl I've met in a long time. You're fresh and real and honest."

Jenny began to smile, and Tri ordered more coffee. When they had drunk it, they walked the four miles back to campus. It was a cool September night, fall was in the air and the leaves were beginnning to turn. The street lights lined the streets with red and yellow shadows from the trees, Tri kept his arm around her to keep her warm, and Jenny thought, as she breathed in the cool night air and felt Tri's sweatered arm at her waist, "I think I have fallen in love."

They met every day in the classroom, the cafeteria, in the library. Tri came for her at the dormitory, and Jenny was waiting at the window. "I just don't see what you've got going, honey," Gayle would say, shaking her head as Jenny dressed, watching out the window for Tri and writing her English Comp. at the same time. "I just don't understand."

On the weekends Tri went home, and Jenny was miserable. She sat alone in the library, she lay in bed in the dormitory. She walked in the park, she looked at her books, she wrote a letter home, but most of all she wondered who the girl was that Tri went home every Saturday to see. She was in love with him and she didn't want to lose sight of him for a minute, let alone two whole days and nights. She dreaded the thoughts of Christmas— three weeks without him. She might lose him during those three weeks, and to lose him would be to lose every reason she had for being alive.

One Monday morning Tri was waiting for her as she came running down the steps of the dormitory.

"Jenny," he said. "Jenny, I'm back." He kissed her cheek and they hurried together down the path.

"I see you are, Tri," Jenny said. "But I wish you'd never gone away."

"I won't any more, honey," he said, putting his arm around her waist and squeezing her close to him. "Without you, that is."

"What do you mean, Tri?"

"Look, honey, I want you to go with me next weekend."

"Go with you?"

"Yes, home. To meet the family. Will you come?"

"Tri," Jenny said. "Oh, Tri, yes!"

The week dragged by. Even the hours spent with Tri went slowly and Jenny thought she would burst before Saturday morning came. She had her bag packed, and Gayle had checked everything in it twice to make sure that old Jenny—old hokey, she called her now as a sort of private joke—hadn't forgotten anything she would need.

Tri came for her in the rain and they caught the bus to Memphis. Gayle waved them out of the bus station and drove herself back to campus in Frank's car. "I just don't understand it," she said to herself, and then to Frank. "What's old Hokey got going for her?"

"Beats me," Frank said. "But I wish I had some."

"Oh, Frank," Gayle said, and hit him with her Algebra book.

When they reached Memphis, Tri's mother was waiting in a new Ford. She said hello to Jenny, gave her a kiss on the cheek, and then hugged Tri.

"So you're Jenny," Alma South sighed on the drive home. "Well, this is wonderful. It's so good to meet you. We've not heard anything but Jenny this and Jenny that all fall. Now we're actually getting to meet you. Honey, this is wonderful."

Tri's home was a split-level house in the suburbs. Jenny met his father, his brothers, his sisters, and felt at home at once. She helped put dinner on the table and then she helped clear away the dishes. She talked in the kitchen with Tri's mother, she laughed and joked with his sisters, and when she went to bed in the guest room that night, her head was swimming with laughter and excitement so that she forgot to leave a light on.

The next morning Tri and his family were waiting for her when she came down to breakfast. "Happy Sunday, honey," Tri said, and put his arm around her. His parents laughed, and his sisters giggled. His brothers punched her in the ribs and the littlest one, who was only three, sat in her lap with his arms around her.

Jenny was happier than she had ever been in all her life. She knew that she loved Tri, she loved his family, and she knew that everything was going to be all right for them. And then Tri told her that he was Catholic and it was time for him to go to Mass. Did she want to go along or stay behind?

She thought that she was going to faint. She felt the bottom slipping out of her world, she felt her feet ready to give way and her head swimming. She was glad that she was sitting down. She hugged the baby to her and dug her head into his back. What could she say? What should she do?

When Tri saw her crying he put his arms around her, right there in front of his parents. "Honey, it's all right," he said. "We're liberated people. This isn't the Middle Ages. It doesn't matter to me what you are. You know how I feel about you. Does it really matter to you where I go to say my prayers?"

The way he put it, the way he said it, right there in front of his parents and his brothers and sisters, with his arms around her, made Jenny feel really ashamed for the first time in her life. She felt that she had really let herself down, and Tri, and his family and her own. She felt little and mean. "Oh, Tri," she said.

"Honey, we don't care what you are," Alma South said. "We're just glad that you're a church-going girl."

"Oh, Tri, I do love you," Jenny said, and she began to cry again.

"I never thought you'd say it," Tri said, swinging her out of the chair and holding her tight. "I never thought you would."

The Souths were laughing and Jenny was crying when Tri asked her to marry him, right there in the kitchen in front of them all.

"Oh, yes, I'll marry you, Tri," Jenny said. "I'll marry you right this minute!"

"Hold on now," Tri said. "Don't you think your folks would want to meet me first?"

On the bus back to Knoxville, sitting up against Tri and smiling to him and to herself, Jenny thought about all the happiness she had found. She thought about how lucky she was. She thought about her home and how lonely she had been there, how lonely she had been last year at Knoxville, and how these past few months had changed her life. She thought about Tri and what a wonderful person he was. She thought about how much she loved him and his family. Then she thought about her own family, and she knew that they would never take him, never love him, never let him be a part of them because of where he said his prayers on Sunday morning.

And so she decided that if Tri wanted to, she would marry him soon, this week even, before he met her family, before she had to take him home with her, or tell him why she couldn't. She would marry him while she could, and be happy while she could. She knew that she couldn't afford to lose a minute of this happiness and she felt that if she let this chance go by, another one would never come.

The next Friday after classes, she and Tri took Frank's car and drove across the county line where they lied about their ages, took a blood test, found a justice of the peace, and were married. They spent the weekend driving up and down the country roads, running through any field they saw and liked long enough to stop by. Jenny kept telling him how beautiful the countryside was in winter time, how beautiful it was when it was cold and dark and bare, how she loved the trees when winter came, and Tri would laugh and say that he was a springtime man himself, he liked it more when the leaves were out and the days were warm and sunny. They laughed and made love in the fields, in the car, in the motel, and came back to campus early Monday morning.

Gayle met Jenny on the steps of the dormitory. "Oh, Jenny," she said. "Oh, Jenny, I'm so glad to see you." And she started to cry.

"What's wrong, Gayle?" Jenny said. "It wasn't as bad as all that."

"Oh, no, Hokey," Gayle said. "They've found out about it."

"Who?"

"Dean Briarley. I don't know how she found out that you were gone, but she did. I tried to cover for you, but she found out. And she found out that Tri was gone, and that you went away together.... I think that your parents must have called."

"Not mine," Jenny said.

"No, yours," Gayle said to Tri. "I don't know how it happened, but they know and they called your parents, Jenny, and they're coming to get you and I think you've been expelled."

Jenny and Tri stood staring through Gayle at the brick dormitory building where Jenny was never going to have to live again as soon as they had enough money to tell everyone that they were married and start living together for sure.

"Oh, Jenny, what are you going to do?" Gayle sobbed. "What are we going to do?"

"I don't know," Jenny said. "I don't know."

"Tri," Gayle started to cry, "Tri..."

"You'd better go on now," Jenny said to Tri. "You'd better get Frank's car back to him. And tell him I said thank you." She smiled at Tri and walked slowly into Madigan Hall.

In the corner of the reception room sat her mother, her father, and Dean Briarley.

"Well, it's about time, young lady," her father said, rising as she came toward them. "It's about time."

"Really, Jenny," Dean Briarley said. "I had not expected this of you."

"Jenny," her mother sobbed. "Oh, Jenny, how could you do this to us?"

"You're a disgrace," her father said. "And you're going home. Your bags are packed and in the car. We've been sitting here waiting for you since six o'clock."

"But Daddy..."

"Running away like that. A scandal. With a man."

"But, Daddy, I..."

"That's enough. How could you have done this to us? We've been here since Sunday morning sitting in the motel and waiting for you. We drove straight through, wondering what in God's name had happened to our little Jenny."

"Really, Mr. Jones, I..."

"Never mind, Dean Briarley. I can tell that you're as distressed as we are."

"Mr. Jones, yes, I am distressed. But this isn't the end of the world. Your daughter is back safe and sound. I hardly think there is any need to take such extreme disciplinary measures. A suspension perhaps... I don't think expulsion is absolute... time to think over her behavior and then return to her classes...such a promising student."

"She'll never set foot out of my house again."

"Mr. Jones, I can hardly concur with this."

"There's no reason for you to concur with it or against it. That's the way it's going to be."

"But, Daddy..."

"Daddy my foot. Get going, girl. We're taking you home."

"But, Daddy, I'm married."

"Oh, Jenny," her mother sobbed.

"No, Jenny," her father said.

"You see, Mr. Jones," Dean Briarley gasped. "I told you that it would all work out. I told you that Jenny was a fine moral girl..." her voice trailed away.

"Married?" Jenny's father turned purple and raised his hands as if to strike her. "Married to that boy? That Catholic?"

"Daddy, I..."

"Oh, yes, we know. We know all about the young man you've been out with. We found out."

"Dean Briarley," Jenny said. "Dean Briarley, how could you."

"I'm sorry, Jenny. We had no reason for not discussing your friends openly with your parents. We were very worried when you disappeared. We questioned your classmates, and they told us of your—relationship—with Mr. South, and we went into his records."

"That Catholic," Jenny's father said again.

"Where were you married, Jenny?" Dean Briarley said.

Jenny told them about her wedding.

"And you must of lied about your age," her father said.

"Yes."

"Well, girl, you're not legally married. And you're going home. Do you understand? And you're not going to see this Tri South again. Ever. Do you understand?"

"Oh, no, Daddy."

"Or you'll break your mother's heart. And mine. And all your family's. We expected something of you, girl. Something besides this. No education and a child every year. Is that what you want? Is it?"

Then she broke down, and started to cry, and her father took her to the car and they drove straight through home.

Once she was back home, back on the ridge, Jenny knew that what she had done was wrong. She knew that God had not intended her to have that kind of life, happily married to a man who was a Catholic and lived far away from the hills of eastern Kentucky. She stayed at home, alone, until she was twenty-one and had gotten over Tri, so she said. She never wrote him and her daddy refused to let him come see her. After a while she didn't grieve any more because she understood that her happiness just wasn't to be. She slept with the light on in the room, and looked out her window at the hills in the moonlight, remembering what it had been like that fall in Knoxville, when she first met Tri and fallen in love with him, when she had gone to see his parents, when they had gotten married and spent that one wonderful weekend driving up and down the country roads, running through the fields and making love.

When she was twenty-one she started taking classes at Maysville Junior College, an hour's drive away from her home. Then she got an emergency certificate and began teaching at Yellowhawk. She taught sixth grade and her students loved her and brought her flowers. They all called her Miss Jones and they all pretended not to know that one time she had run away and gotten married but her daddy had come after her and made her come home again.

❧VII❧

"And I said to her, I said, Letha, you're living in sin. I've not come here to judge you, that's the Lord's duty. But I've come to chastize you. This is my duty, as a sister. I said, Letha, repent yourself unto the Lord and seek His salvation. Then will your sins be forgiven you and you can go on in this life, righteously preparing for the next."

"What'd she say, Zania?"

"She wouldn't listen. She shook her head and told me that if I weren't her husband's sister she'd have ordered me out of the house. Her husband's sister, mind you, and I claim her as my own, believing as I do that we are all one family under the Lord. And then she said I was to talk of something else or leave."

"What'd you do?"

"Well, what could I do? I was inspired to speak of the Lord. I had prayed to Him, and He had answered me and told me to go and convert Letha Miller. But she'd have no part of the Lord or me. She blasphemed God when she told me not to speak of Him. So I left. I went to my car and prayed for forgiveness in failing Him. I prayed hard, then I backed the car out of her driveway and went home."

Zania bowed her head and stared hard at her long, white slender hands. Her thin lips were pulled down tightly over her large white teeth. Her drawn eyelids were smooth and serene, fastidiously protecting the violet eyes from the light of day and the evils of man. Then the bell rang. Zania tossed her black galoshes in the corner, hung her coat on a peg, and walked down the hall to class.

At noon, two eighth graders—girls from Zania France's homeroom—tapped on the door of Mary Savage's room. Miss Savage nodded to them to come in.

"We've come to look at your room," Patty Mercer said shyly.

"If we don't bother you, that is," said Cheryl Bush.

"No, go right ahead."

"We'll be quiet."

The girls tiptoed about, admiring this and that, but most of all the tiny pine tree that stood in the corner. They fingered each chain and paper angel and squinted their eyes to make the glass beads throw off colored lights. Then they talked about the painted wreath on the door and the frieze of Christmas drawings on the art board.

"You sure have got pretty things in here," Patty whispered to Miss Savage.

"Thank you," Mary Savage said. "The students enjoyed making them. So did I."

"What's that they're doing now?"

Miss Savage picked up a piece of snow-white paper and spread it out for the girls to see. "It's a snowflake," she said. "We're making them for the windows."

"How pretty," Cheryl sighed. "Do they take long to do?"

"Most of the noon hour. It's a wonderful way for us to pass the time on these cold snowy days when we can't go outside."

"I guess so."

"Don't these things bother you? Don't they get in your way?" Cheryl asked, stroking the green and gold glitter on the tree decorations.

"The tree, you mean? Of course not. We put it here in the corner where we wouldn't be brushing against it when we passed. We put it here by Tullie's seat. She's in charge of seeing that nothing happens to it."

Tullie looked up from her desk and grinned at the big seventh-grade girls.

Patty and Cheryl lingered on. Their sighs began to distract the students crouched over squares of white folded paper, their sharp eyes designing snowflakes long before their little hands twisted through blunt scissors and began to cut.

"Would you like to show me your room?" Miss Savage asked at last.

"Oh, we can't. I mean, there's nothing in it."

"No Christmas decorations yet?"

"We can't put anything up. Mrs. France doesn't believe in it. It's against her religion."

Mary Savage felt her smooth high cheeks beginning to flush. She bit her lip and was sorry she had asked the girls anything at all about their homeroom. If Zania France found out about it, she would accuse Mary of snooping and prying.

She looked down at her watch and said, "Sorry, girls, but you'll have to go. I have some papers to grade before the bell rings." Patty and Cheryl stood looking at her eagerly, and she could tell by the glint in their eyes that they were eager to talk to her about their teacher. But there were some things, she knew, that it was better not to know about.

Tullie watched the door close, then grinned and motioned Miss Savage to come to her desk, holding up her crooked snowflake which she had colored green.

Miss Savage smiled and went to her. "You've done well, Tullie," she said. "But why did you make it green?"

Tullie chuckled under her breath and swung her long straight hair across her thin face. "A strange one, all right," she said.

"What's that, Tullie?"

Tullie put her mouth up close to Miss Savage's ear and whispered behind her cupped hands, "She's a strange one, Mrs. France is. She had me when I was in the fourth grade. We didn't get along. I'm glad to be out of there. And I won't go back to her next year, neither."

Mary Savage pulled up a little chair and sat down. She began to talk to Tullie about how snowflakes are white, not green, and how Mrs. France was a very fine person who liked Tullie and would be fair and kind to her.

While they were waiting for their bus that afternoon, Patty Mercer and Cheryl Bush began sketching snowflakes on a piece of plain typing paper divided up between them.

"Was this the way it looked?" Patty asked.

"I think so. But she folded it some way, then cut."

"Can't you remember how they did it?"

"No, can you?"

"No. Do you think we could ask her?"

"Go next door, you mean?"

"Yes. She wouldn't mind."

Patty raised her hand and asked permission to go next door.

"What for?" asked Zania France.

"I want to ask Miss Savage something."

"She doesn't need to be bothered. She's got work to do. What do you want?"

"Oh, nothing, thank you," Patty slid back into her seat.

Zania France felt a clock ticking its warning somewhere inside her heart. She heard the voice of God speaking to her, and she said, "Girls, what are you doing?"

Patty and Cheryl held up their snowflakes.

Zania France's lips tightened. Her face turned red, her kinky permanented hair frizzled across her forehead. "I've told you," she whispered, her voice down low, "I've told you not to do that in here. I've told you that this is a room for study and work. Haven't you got anything useful to do?"

"Yes, ma'am," the girls said, pulling out their school books.

"Then do it. And don't let me catch you at this again. Ever." Zania France wadded up the two snowflakes and tossed them into the wastebasket. Then, shaking with anger, she went to call on Mary Savage down the hall.

"I just don't like it," Zania said, leaning down close to Mary Savage and shaking her frizzy head. "I just don't like it one bit. When could they have sneaked into your room?"

"What do you mean?"

"Patty Mercer and Cheryl Bush is what I mean. They must of sneaked into your room."

"They didn't sneak in here, Zania," Mary said. "They came in when I was here working."

"Oh," Zania stared hard at Mary, who wore eye makeup and whom she did not like at all. "You mean you let them in?"

"Of course."

"Don't you know there's no visiting allowed at the noon hour?"

Mary shrugged. "It was a snowy day. They asked to come in. I saw no harm ..."

"You saw no harm?" Zania sputtered. "You saw no harm? Well, there was harm done. Dirty, filthy, degrading harm done to their little minds. But it's torn up and thrown away now, praise God. It's lying in the wastebasket to be burned to perdition."

Mary waved a hand at Zania, as if asking her for an explanation.

"Them drawings," Zania said. "Them drawings, them evil drawings. They saw them. They're trying to copy them."

"Oh, you mean the snowflakes, Zania. That's all right." Mary couldn't keep from smirking. "I don't mind if we have the same decorations in our rooms ... I don't mind if you don't."

"Oh, but I do," Zania hissed. "I do mind, awful much. I don't want any decoration in my room. I won't have it. It's evil. It's spoiling the natural beauty of the Lord. It's corrupting them with colors and lustful shapes and grand ideas of doing something in their spare time besides working and praising the Lord. I don't like it, do you hear? And I won't have it. So you keep them out and you keep your door closed. I don't even want them seeing your room." She turned on her heel and marched back into her room, slamming the door behind her.

Stunned, Mary Savage stood as if rooted to the concrete floor. She did not hear the bus boy announce the Milk Moon Run. She did not see Tullie scamper down the hall, clutching a paper chain in one hand and her spelling book in the other, as she beat it out the door to start her own way home, always managing to get there before the bus driver dropped off the other children who lived at Easter Gap. But she did hear Tullie call to her, "I told you so," and point to Zania France's closed door.

Zania France drove home easily, slowly, at peace with herself. "I did the right thing," she thought happily. "I protected God. And myself. And the uncorrupted minds of the sweet innocents I teach." She hummed a hymn under her breath and wondered if she would have enough time for a bath before prayer meeting. "I doubt it," she decided. "I've got to get my chemistry done."

The classes she met twice a week at Maysville Jr. College were hard on her. Math and chemistry had been hard enough in high

school, but college was another thing. But she would master
them! The Lord was behind her. The Lord knew she had chosen
plain subjects, subjects that had not been infiltrated by fanciness
and corruption. Math to her was in theory as simple as the road
to Heaven—once you found the way, you stuck to it. And it got
you there. It got Zania high C's in both her sophomore courses,
and this was enough for the time being. She had a husband and
two boys to cope with, too. Besides Yellowhawk. It was hard
keeping everyone on the straight and narrow path. It was hard
opening their eyes to the glories of the Lord, and closing them
to the evils of man.

Conk was waiting for her at the hollow road.

"Hi, Mom," he cried, sliding into the seat beside her.

She ruffled his hair with her right hand. "Good day at school?"
she asked.

"Yeah. O.K." His face fell. "It was O.K. I passed the English
test. Just barely, but I passed it."

"Good."

"I could of done better if you'd let me study more."

"Not poetry, Conk," Zania said firmly. "You know you're not
to study poetry."

"Yes, ma'am."

Zania studied his troubled face. "Anything else to tell me?"

Conk handed her a note. "It's from Miss Barclay," he said. "To
you."

"Do you know what it's about?"

"Yes, ma'am."

"What, Conk?"

"The pledge of allegiance. She wants to know why I won't say
it."

"Did you explain to her?"

"Yes, ma'am."

"I told her that my pledge was made unto God. That when I
honored Him, I honored His country. That I would not take the
oath to anything or anyone but God," Conk droned away in a
sing-song voice.

"That's fine, Conk," Zania said, pleased. "What did Miss
Barclay say?"

"Nothing. She just wrote you this note."

"Put it in my pocket, Conk. I'll read it when I get home."

Prayer meeting was inspiring. Zania felt the word of God enter into her heart. She meditated for a long while on her hard wooden bench before she lifted up her voice in song with her husband Ed and the boys Conk and Albert. When she did sing, she held her face high, her violet eyes fixed hard on the preacher's face. Little drops of perspiration fixed themselves to the roots of her frizzy hair and drizzled down her plain, unpowdered face. Drops of moisture formed at the corner of her eyes and trickled to her lips.

Ed groped for his handkerchief and held it out to her. Like one fixed in a trance, she did not see him, or the handkerchief or her two sons watching curiously. Finally, Ed himself wiped off her face.

"Let her be, brother," Old Mollie Appleton whispered to Ed, tapping his shoulder for attention. "Let her be. It's a sign that God's within her."

Ed nodded to old Mollie and pulled his hand away, stuffing the sweaty cloth back into his pocket.

Zania prayed and sang with all the fervor in her thin body. With difficulty she kept her arms pinned close to her sides—they seemed like bright thin beams of energy, anxious to leap forward, to sway and fall and fling themselves to the rhythm of the music of God. Her small feet, stuffed into the muddy shoes she wore, tapped lightly on the wood floor. Those feet were unaware of the cold freezing air that leaked through the wooden cracks of the church house and chilled them until they swelled. Those feet were bright stars of energy, ready to burn out their ecstasy to the music.

A funny thought ran through Ed's mind: "If there were snakes around, she'd pick them up and fondle them." Horrified by his blasphemy, he sank back into the pew and prayed God to forgive him. What could have made him think that? Zania was a true believer. She'd have no idols. She would not need to prove her devotion, her fearlessness, through serpents.

Or would she? The thought would not leave his mind. Would she recoil from the curling, winding, pus-inflamed bodies? Or would she reach out willingly, eagerly, calling them to her because they were blessed, a part of her family, a portion of the earth and a part of the creatures named in the holy book and blessed by God.

In the back of her head, Zania saw Ed slumped to the bench. Her heart rejoiced. Her body exulted. She lifted up her hands and stretched them high, high toward God, to thank Him for touching her husband so powerfully. She often reproached Ed for his lack of emotion in the church. But now, tonight, he too was caught up. He had sniffed the mystic flavor of heaven, he was tasting right now of its glory fruits. "Thank You, God," Zania prayed. And then the spell was broken—she saw that it was time to go. Her boys were asleep, curled up beside her; Ed was still silent, his head bowed, the awful thought tormenting him. But Zania, Zania was at peace with God and man. She lifted Ed's arm and was surprised to see his entire body rise, weightless, beneath her firm grasp.

"It's time to go," she said.

"Yes," he replied numbly.

"The spirits were with you."

"Yes."

In the car, with Albert on her lap and Conk stretched out in the back seat, she smiled at Ed. She loved him for this. She loved him for sharing with her her emotions, the deep feelings she had felt in church tonight. "Tonight," she thought, "tonight, if he— if he wants me—maybe I can bring myself to do it. It will be hard, but maybe I can. Not to repay him for loving God, but to show him that I try to share his feelings, too." She bowed her head and began to pray again. She would need strength.

But Ed was too tired to do anything but fall asleep, or pretend to sleep. That strange, evil thought was still flourishing in his mind, tempting him, taunting him, making him probe to the depths of his being to see what had made him think such a thing. "Could it be the devil?" he wondered. "Has he got me at last because he knows that I'm an unbeliever?"

He shuddered and turned to Zania for warmth. But her body was to him like a huge, bloated snake, curled up and resting on her pillow. He recoiled. He sat up, the sweat beading on his forehead and oozing down his face in steady streams.

"I can't sleep, either," Zania said. "They're still with you, aren't they? The spirits?"

"Yes," Ed said hoarsely.

"Sometimes they get me, too. Sometimes I can't sleep either. I'm too fired up with the glory of God. I'm too thrilled at hearing His voice. I can't go to sleep. I can't risk having that echo in my ears grow dimmer."

"No."

"Why don't you walk?" Zania asked drowsily. "A walk might do you good. Go contemplate the night."

The cold air, Ed thought, the cold air. He began to dress, pulling on his heavy boots and coat and scarf. It was winter out, but he must go.

He took the Hubbard Hollow route. He was a man with a purpose, a man drawn to the southern hills. He hurried to the field of flat rocks where copperheads hibernated in the winter. Under one of those thick rocks, he knew, was a drowsy snake, waiting to be taken home, to be revived by the warmth of the barn hay and the fire.

Zania was tired on Friday. She was worn out from her frenzy at prayer meeting. She looked pale and bedraggled to her students. Her frizzy hair flopped in her face, and she made no attempt to push it back. She put in the hours at school, but she had no energy, no interest. She gave the students busy work when they ran out of seat assignments.

At noon, she called Miss Barclay and talked to her about Conk. But she was soft, almost gentle with the unbeliever. She had no desire to explain, to chastize, to make her religion known. She had no real interest in Miss Barclay, or in Miss Barclay's soul. For some reason, she felt that today God could look after His own.

Lois Barclay was surprised to find at the other end of the line an intelligent-sounding young woman who seemed calm and understanding instead of the fanatic fireball she had been warned not to tangle with. So Lois Barclay tried to be calm and understanding too, gentle and considerate instead of firm and matter of fact, the way she had intended to be. To Miss Barclay's surprise, Zania agreed to meet her some afternoon and discuss further the harm that Lois Barclay felt Conk's attitude was doing him. Zania listened listlessly while Lois Barclay explained that it was—un-usual—for a boy Conk's age to be so deeply religious, in an—unconventional (she chose her words carefully)—way. "I some-times get the feeling that the other students are avoiding him because they think he's...strange."

Zania didn't even bother to tell Lois Barclay that the Lord was the only companion needed by man or child.

The drive to college took about two hours. Zania was glad it was her turn to ride. She squeezed herself in a place in the back and stared out the window, instead of studying as she always did on the drive. Her classmates, eating their Colonel Sanders chicken dinners and talking with each other, noticed that Zania was sure acting strange tonight. But they thought no more about it. Zania was strange anyway.

Coming home, she thought little about chemistry or math. She knew she had done badly in the quizzes her professors had given. She would have to study much harder to make up her average. She had to get her degree and get qualified soon. If she didn't, the state might not give her any more emergency-teaching certificates. She had already taught five years on one and a half years of college and emergency-teaching certificates. What if she couldn't get any more? What if there was some kind of rule? What if she lost her job?

Somehow, all this did not get through to her. She kept her eye fixed on the moon, her face pressed to the windowpane. "What's happening to me?" she wondered. "What's happening inside?"

She tried to analyze her feelings, but she couldn't. She was going to need all her strength, she felt instinctively, to meet what was coming. She could feel a strange presence inside her. It was a warning. So she closed her eyes and slept.

Ed watched his wife undress and throw on her modest night-gown. She hung her dress carefully in the closet, folded her sweater and tucked it into the drawer. She dusted off her shoes and stood them on the floor by her dresser. Then she turned her back and slipped off her underwear under the gown.

Ed watched her nervously. His face was cold, frightened, motionless. He sat in his chair, fiddling with the lacings on his boots. "What have I done?" went spinning through his mind. "What have I done?"

With great effort, Zania turned down the covers. First the quilt, which she folded double and lay at the foot of the bed. Then the comforter. Then the sheet. As she reached over to puff her pillow, as she always did, she saw the snake.

A great trembling went through her body. Her head was thrown back and her violet eyes permeated the ceiling of the house, and the black sky itself, in search for God and for understanding. Then, knowingly, she turned to Ed. "You," she whispered. "You, whom the devils have infested. Last night it was God fighting for you. Today it was the devil. It is up to me who will win you. Isn't that right?"

Ed shook his head.

"You need a sign," Zania mumbled to herself. "A sign." She stood very still, very straight, very erect. She was gaining power over herself. She was conquering her fear, fear which would give off scent that would feed into the serpent's breathing tongue, fear that would make him strike.

Then, with rigid arms that did not tremble, with supple hands that curved gently about his slick greasy body, Zania scooped up the copperhead from its resting place in her bed. "Come," she whispered to him softly. "Come, little snake. Come, beloved of the Lord. Yours is the earth, but not my bed. Go, crawl in the night, where you belong." She carried the snake easily, drawn up to her bosom. She neither clutched nor crushed him. One soothing hand rested over his head.

"Come," she whispered.

Ed's eyes followed her across the room. He watched her free one hand to open the door. He saw her bend down gracefully and let the serpent loose. Then, she turned and looked back at him. Her violet eyes compelled him. With a sickening feeling slipping up his throat, he slid from the chair to his knees and began to pray.

❧VIII❧

After his bike broke down, Stubby Jones gave in and started walking the last six or seven miles home to The Gap. Not that he minded getting his feet off the pedals and back down on the hard ground. His black leather ankle boots knocked the clods of frozen dirt and grass aside, and his big blue-jeaned legs pushed against the stiff broomsedge and underbrush growing thick across the road. He took off his gloves and let his smooth, short, stubby basketball hands pull at the wind, he threw back his neck and looked up. Even the thin blue strips of sky pasted between rough boulders of clouds were thinning out, giving way to a dry brittle grayness that went, with the cold, down his throat and into the pit of his stomach.

Stubby had figured that the bike wouldn't make it. He'd only had a hundred and fifty dollars to spend, though, and what could you buy for a hundred and fifty dollars any more? A Honda 90 with 3,000 miles, a double seat to ride the girls around, and a new chrome rack to tie your duffle bag to. It was too bad, though, that he'd made it this far, and then had to see it break down. Now he'd have to hitch a ride back to the gas station where he'd parked it, and figure some way to get the thing to his home, so he could fix it up in time to ride back to Tennessee. And his dad wouldn't like it at all. His dad had told him once that if he was going to buy himself a hell cycle and break his neck like some hick idiot that he needn't bother to come home.

"Stubby," his father had said, "there won't be a place for you with your brothers. You're the oldest, and you've got to set the way. You've got to show the boys that someone from The Gap can amount to something. You've got to be somebody. You know what I mean?"

"Yessir."

"Sure now?"

"Yessir."

"That's the only way to do things any more. You've got to stand up for yourself, and be an individual. You've got to be a loner. I don't mean don't have any friends. But don't get too close to anybody. Don't let them know what you're thinking. Stand off to yourself and see it all with your own eyes. Make up your own mind. I've raised you right, I've shown you the best way I could find. Maybe that won't be the way for you. I hope it is—but if it isn't, I'll try to understand. Maybe you'll find a better way than your old dad. Maybe you'll dig gold, instead of potatoes."

So Stubby had gone off to junior college on a basketball scholarship and the money he had saved from filling brown paper bags at the checkout counter and carrying the groceries out to cars. He'd gone with one suitcase to put in the rack of the Greyhound bus, and he'd seen the other kids laugh as they loaded on their trunks and kept their Smith-Corona typewriters at their feet. Once the bus pulled away from the Beeville Station, and their mothers were out of sight, the girls moved to the back and lighted up filter cigarettes and turned on their transistor radios. Stubby Jones was surprised and a little embarrassed to see them acting this way. They reminded him of junior-high girls on the bus for their first trip over to Carson to go shopping on a Saturday afternoon. He hadn't thought that college girls would be like that.

He'd had two letters from his mom that fall, both of them asking for news, both of them white sheets of paper wrapped around a five-dollar bill. Stubby felt funny about the money. He put it aside and didn't use it. Now that he had a cafeteria job, he didn't need the extra, and he didn't want to take what his mom had saved back. It's not that they were poor, Stubby said to himself, as he put the money under his white dress shirt, it's just that they weren't the type to spend what they made. It's not that they were misers, either. Big Bill Jones had kept his tithe to the Methodist Church for the past seven or eight years.

Stubby didn't know exactly what to call his home until his

sociology professor began to lecture about lower- and upper-middle-class farming families and conservatism. At first, just listening to the way the professor talked made Stubby's blood boil, and he knew that his face was red as he gripped the sides of his seat to keep from stuttering out in his anger. Then, as the classes went on, Stubby began to be able to listen without feeling that he was being insulted. He saw himself being put into a category, a little bit out in front of his mom and dad, but not much. And, like the real Gap that had separated him from his playmates at Yellowhawk—the five-mile walk down to school and up the hill home, through brush that would never, never be cleared to let a schoolbus through—he now saw the big gaps between him and his other classmates. It wasn't so much the money, or the way they were dressed, or what they did on Friday nights that made the difference. It was their way of thinking. It was the way they answered the questions Professor Lewis asked them; it was the things they thought of to say on their own. It was a difference, Stubby thought, that must have been born in them and fed with the words and thoughts of their growing years. Their minds had been shaped differently, just as their bodies. Stubby knew that he loomed up like a storybook corn-fed farm boy, and he blushed when the girls stared at him hard between classes.

"I never did see one as tall as that," he heard one long-blonde-haired girl stage whisper to her friend. And the other girl laughed, her eyes very bright as she smiled up at him. But all Stubby could think about, when he looked down at them, was what made them so small? TV dinners and diet cokes? What about their heads, he wondered. Had they been starved, too?

His grades hadn't been that good, according to his mid-term reports. He had kept up his high school B, with a C+ in sociology. But it didn't bother him, not even when Professor Lewis asked him to come by his office.

"I think," Professor Lewis said to him, "that you have a good head on your shoulders. And I think that you are beginning to use it. Did anyone ever teach you how to think?"

"No, sir," Stubby said. "Well, yes, sir. I guess my dad did."

"I see. What did he talk to you about?"

"What I ought to do with myself."

"Did he have anything in mind?"

"Not exactly. He just said I ought to make something out of myself. Be different."

"Are you the oldest?"

"Yes, sir. I guess I'm supposed to set an example for the others."

Professor Lewis nodded and offered him a cigarette. Stubby said no thank you.

"I forget," Professor Lewis said, shaking his head apologetically, "you're in training."

"Yes, sir."

"You know, Stubby," Professor Lewis said, "I wouldn't want to go against your training, but you don't have to keep saying 'yes, sir' and 'no, sir' to me. Everybody welcomes a little respect, but you don't have to treat me like I have all the answers and your fate is hanging in my hands. I didn't call you in here to talk about your grade. I don't even remember what I gave you on your mid-term report, but I don't think it was too good. But that isn't important. You'll learn how to study and write down the correct answers soon enough. You'll be making all A's once you've learned to type a teacher and you figure out just what he wants you to say, and throw it all back in his face in neat writing in your blue book. What I wanted to do was talk to you. You don't say much in class, but I don't think it's because you're not listening. I think you're afraid. I just wanted to tell you not to be. You'll learn how to express yourself as well as your classmates once you start trying. Just speak up now and then and say what you think. And don't be upset if someone doesn't agree with you, or if I tell you I think you're completely off base. After all, it's not always a question of right and wrong. Sometimes it's just your ideas and mine. It's just communication that we're trying for."

Stubby left the office and went on to basketball practice. What Professor Lewis had said didn't surprise him much. Somehow, he had felt that his teacher was going to say that. He had seen it in his eyes, and he had heard it in the way Lewis twisted his pencil before he said a word.

Stubby had the feeling that Professor Lewis knew a lot about him. More than the things he saw just by looking at him—his poor clothes, his hands rough and red from washing dishes, his eyes a little tired from studying late after the ball games. More than the things that were on his record—his father's name and occupation, the poor county he came from, his years at Yellow-hawk, his high school activities. The Professor knew more than all this, more of the things that were going on inside his head. Stubby felt that he was just now beginning to think, and that the sounds of his thoughts getting started and taking speed were very loud and hard to teach over. Professor Lewis hadn't said anything when Stubby said his father had taught him how to think. Pro-fessor Lewis knew the kinds of thoughts Big Bill Jones had. They were the kind of thoughts everyone had had thirty years ago. There wasn't anything wrong with them, Stubby hurried to add to himself. He wasn't making a value judgment on them. They just weren't relevant any more. Here he was, Stubby Jones from the high Gap at the corner of east Kentucky, in a little junior college in Tennessee on a basketball scholarship...in the age of *Time* magazine and men on the moon and somewhere a hippie generation carrying flowers and talking about love. And it all meant nothing to him. To be something any more meant to be a part of all this. In the new world, you just didn't wash dishes to get through school or nudge another man out to make the basket and get the point and get your scholarship renewed. You just didn't do it, but here he was, Stubby Jones, and he was doing it.

He thought about it all, as he walked down the creek bank out of the road. The bus was going by, but he didn't want to be on it. It would be full of silly girls and red-faced boys on their way home for Christmas. These would be the girls who hadn't got any boy friends to drive them home, and the boys who didn't have the money for cars. He didn't want to be a part of them. He'd bought a bike so he could get around by himself, and the bike had broken down. Now he had that to explain to his dad, and he knew his mom would stand in the kitchen, frowning, and his dad would get very angry and say he'd gone to hell, and what was the use of his going away to school if he wasn't going to make any-thing out of himself.

The creek was frozen, and Stubby felt his feet beginning to get cold. He put his gloves back on, and took his scarf out of his little bag and wound it around his neck. A cup of coffee would taste good now. It wouldn't be much farther. In spite of his fears, he felt himself getting eager to be back home. His mother would be in the kitchen, probably opening home-canned peaches for a cobbler, and his brothers would be shooting their basketball through the hoop nailed up to the side of the barn. He thought he'd slip by the shed and pick up a load of wood for the fireplace and carry it in through the back door. "Is that you, Bill?" his mother would say, and he would answer, "No, it's just me." He could see the surprise on his mother's face, and it made him laugh and hurry his steps.

Up ahead, at the bend in the road, Stubby saw an old pick-up truck pulled off at the side with the hood opened up. A man was bending down over it, fooling with the insides. "I wonder who that is," Stubby said aloud. His breath turned white in the air. "I thought I knew all the cars around here. Must be somebody passing through. He's got a cold job there."

Just for a minute, he wondered if he would stop and offer to help. It might mean getting home an hour or two later and a lot colder. His folks would be worried about him by then. He'd written then that he'd be in by suppertime Saturday. He didn't want his mom upset, and dinner cold. He knew it would be a special dinner. And if his father were hungry and out of humor, it would be a lot harder to talk to him about the motorcycle.

The man looked up, saw the boy walking by the creekbed, and waved. Stubby couldn't hear his words. He was far enough away from the wind to carry them out of reach. But he heard them in his head—"Hello, there, can you give me a hand?"

Yes, I'm coming, he thought, as he climbed up the frozen bank and went toward the bend. I'll try to fix it up and get a ride home. If I can fix it, that is. That truck's in the worst shape I've seen for a long time. It looks worse than my bike. Who on earth would buy something like that—he must be crazier than I am.

"Sure is good to see you, fellow." He could hear the man's voice now. "I thought I was stranded out here for sure. It's almost dark and I can't lock her up. Just been to town and I've got to get this load home. Thought I'd be out here the night. Wouldn't like to do that, either. I've got a boy coming home from college today. Haven't seen him in almost three months. I sure would appreciate it if you could have a look under the hood. I can't tell what's wrong. But then I'm not much of a mechanic."

Stubby just stared at the man, who kept on talking excitedly as he came closer.

"Good Lord, Dad,'" he said, finally, when he could get his breath. And he started to laugh.

Big Bill Jones looked up from under the hood of the Ford. "Stubby," he said, and his face was red from cold and surprise. "Stubby. What on earth are you doing out here?"

"Well, you just wouldn't believe it, Dad," Stubby said, pulling at his gloves. "And after this walk, I don't, either. Let's see what I can do for this, first, and I'll tell you about it later."

Stubby stuck his head down over the engine and then looked up at his father. "Is this truck yours—I mean, ours?"

"I'm afraid so, son. I needed it for the farm, you know. I didn't make a very good buy. In fact, I got a real lemon. I guess I should have waited for you to come home and help me pick one out."

"I don't know, Dad," Stubby said, laughing.

"What do you mean?"

Stubby looked at his father. "I've learned a lot in three months at college," he said. "But I've still got a lot to learn."

"Well, that's nothing, boy," Bill Jones said, and he started laughing, too. "I've been at it for fifty-five years, and you see the mess I'm in."

It took an hour and a half to fix the truck. When he got the engine going, Stubby put his father inside to get warm. Then he climbed up beside him and said, "Where to?"

"Where do you think?" his father asked. "Your mother is going to be half out of her mind. Do you want to drive?"

His father had never let him drive the family car.

"No," Stubby said. "My hands are too cold. You'd better."

Bill Jones smiled and pulled out on the road. "It's really a great little truck," he said. "Goes right through the fields. We can take the short way home."

And he drove up the hill where Stubby had walked, sure

within himself that the bush would never part to let a bus or truck go through.

By the time they reached the tobacco base, Stubby had told his dad all about the Honda, how he had ridden it until he was within eight miles of home, and then it had broken down with him.

"Why didn't you give us a call?" Bill said. "We would have come for you. No need for you to walk all that way."

Stubby turned his head so his father couldn't see his face. He couldn't tell him the truth, that he had wanted to drive up on his bike so his father could see that a motorcycle wasn't so bad; that he had wanted to impress them all by coming home that way, alone, and show it off to his brothers, and really be somebody. He couldn't tell his father that he had been afraid that he wouldn't understand, and he didn't want to get a lecture the first night he was home, there in front of his brothers and his mother.

But his father was smiling now, as he drove the rattlely little truck across the flat of The Gap. "I think I know your reasons, boy," he said. "And I can tell you, it wouldn't have been that way. You didn't tell me what a Honda is, but I know it's a motorcycle. And I can tell by the looks of you that you've not changed. For the bad, I mean. I know I've said a lot of opinionated things before, but I thought I always told you that our ways might be different. If you want to drive that Honda, Stubby, it's up to you. I'm not saying I approve, or disapprove. Look, since you've been gone, I've learned some things, too. I've learned that it's not so much what you drive—it depends upon the man behind the wheel. If you only knew how many times this truck has broken down on me."

"I'll see what I can do for it while I'm home," Stubby said.

"I sure would appreciate that."

They were pulling up to the barn. "I always park it inside," Big Bill said.

Stubby got out to open the barn doors. It was colder now, and the sky was black, with just a few stars and a very full moon. The lights were on in the house, smoke was coming from the chimney, and he saw the front door open, and heard his mother call, "Is that you, Bill? Stubby's not home yet."

"It's me," his father shouted back. "Don't worry about Stubby." He winked at his son. "Let's give her a surprise," he said.

"All right."

They bolted the doors and started up the path. "You'd better drive the truck over and pick up your bike tomorrow," he said. "I wouldn't want to leave it out among strangers, if I were you. And I can manage with the car—unless you want me to go with you, that is. I don't have anything that has to be done tomorrow."

"That would be fine," Stubby said.

"We might even take your mother," Bill said. "She'd enjoy the ride."

And Stubby laughed when his mother saw them coming up the path together, laughed hard at the thoughts of his mom sitting in the cabin of the truck while he and his dad sweated and shoved to push his broken-down black bike into the bed of that worn-out truck.

IX

Hilda Redfern had big ivory teeth that stuck out of her mouth
at an angle and earned her the name Horsey Hilda. She always
made Roy think of some of the characters in a deck of Old Maid.
Only she looked like more than one—she had Spinster Sally's
prim drawn-up face and Goofy Grace's happy way of smiling at
you when she wanted to say hello. She even reminded Roy of
Pistol Pete, although he was a man card, by the way she walked,
a little bow-legged, and Roy could always imagine her twirling a
lasso, which made him laugh so hard he had to put my hand over
his mouth so she wouldn't see him looking at her and laughing.

Hilda always came to town on Saturdays to get her mail, buy
her groceries, and shop for whatever odds and ends she needed at
the hardware. She kept long detailed lists—Roy had seen her looking them over when she did her grocery shopping—which she
studied, marked through, and wrote notes beside as she checked
over the merchandise on her Saturday jaunts. Roy had always liked
Hilda, and he liked to cart out her groceries and pile them in the
back of her Ford. She always gave him a quarter; she never forgot,
even when Iris McQuarter was across the street, and she was
so caught up looking at him that it was all she could do to get
the back door open for Roy to load the groceries in her Ford.

They said that Hilda had always been sweet on Iris but he
wouldn't have anything to do with her because she was so ugly.
Roy himself didn't think that was true, but then like they told him,
what does a fourteen-year-old boy know about what makes a
woman ugly or beautiful. But Roy liked old Hilda and he liked
watching her read over her lists while she stood on the sidewalk
peeping over the top of her paper to watch Iris McQuarter.

Iris was basketball coach at Independent high school and

he was so proud that his school had never joined in the county system that he wouldn't even have anything to do with the county teachers. That let Hilda out right there because she was the fourth-grade teacher at Yellowhawk, and she was proud of her school because it was, according to Hilda, the number-one elementary school in the county.

She used to tell Roy that every Saturday when she was doing her grocery shopping. She would tell him that he ought to be proud that he went to Yellowhawk and that he ought not to let anybody talk him into going to Independent high school when he could go to the county schools for free and they were so much better anyway. Roy heard it all from Hilda so many times that he finally said to her once, "Well, Miss Redfern, I reckon I will go to Independent anyway because I want to play basketball for Coach McQuarter because he's my cousin and I know I can get on the team."

Hilda looked him over with a new respect. "Your cousin?" she said, checking tomato paste off her list.

"That's right," Roy said. "And I can get on the team because it's so small that they need every man they can get. But if I go to the County, I'll never get to play basketball because there are so many boys there taller than me. And I don't want to be on the B team and have to sit it out until we whop the daylights out of Independent. I'd rather be on the Independent A team and get beaten all over the court than sit it out in the B-team county rows."

"Roy," Hilda said, "you've got a good head on your shoulders after all. What are you doing working in a grocery store?"

"It's good money, Miss Redfern," Roy said. "Fifty cents an hour and my tips. I can use the money."

"Can't we all," Hilda said, throwing a can of apple juice in the cart.

Then she looked through the plate-glass windows of the grocery store and saw Iris McQuarter across the street talking to the men in the square. "Just think," she said, "what a person could do here with two salaries."

That's the way Hilda thought. She was determined right from the beginning to get her hands on Iris McQuarter. She wanted him to marry her, Roy knew it all along. She wanted to be Hilda

Redfern McQuarter, living in town and not on the old farm she kept up in Bright April Valley. And she wanted to live on two salaries so she could eat well, drive a good car, and have money to spend on some better-looking clothes. Roy knew that's the way Hilda thought because he heard his sisters say so, and if there's anybody who can figure out what another woman is after, especially when it comes to a man, it's Roy's sisters. They were all in high school in the County except Caroline, who was married, and they were already looking out for their old age, when they would need men to support them and keep them in hair curlers and cold cream.

But old Hilda was smarter than Roy's sisters. She had ten or fifteen years on them and she had been working to catch Iris ever since she graduated from high school and went to junior college. But she couldn't catch him, no matter what she did or how she tried, so she went on to night school and finished up her diploma and got herself certified. That put her up high on the school-board payroll and people started looking up to Hilda in spite of themselves. She was one of the first teachers in the county to have a real college education and be certified by the State of Kentucky.

About this time Iris McQuarter got married to Ethel Sparks and Hilda set her big ivory teeth together and disappeared for a while. She quit teaching, took her savings out of the bank, and went away. She was gone a year, and, when she came back to do her grocery shopping, she told Paul Lee, who worked at the grocery and dared Roy's oldest sister, that she had been to the University of Kentucky and got herself a Master's Degree in Education. Now she made even more money, and Mr. Jenkins, her principal, was afraid that he was going to lose her to one of the high schools. He was really afraid that Independent High would hire her, because Independent had more money to pay and was looking for better teachers.

Roy didn't know if Hilda tried to get a job there or not, but when September came, she was back at Yellowhawk with her fourth graders. She taught there for another year, and then found out that Iris and his wife Ethel were going to have a baby. She disappeared again, this time for a couple of years, and the county said she had gone out of her head from grief, but she was a fine woman and didn't want to spoil anything for Iris and his wife, and that was the right thing for her to do. The county liked her because she was a good loser. When Hilda came back she was thinner and had some gray hairs, and her big teeth had sort of settled back into her mouth at an angle. That's when Roy's sisters nicknamed her Horsey Hilda and the name caught on. Roy met Hilda in the grocery store where he had started working and, when she asked about Paul Lee, Roy told her he had graduated from high school and started selling insurance. Roy told her that he was working in Paul's place, and she said he looked too young for that.

That's when Roy told her that he needed the money and she started in at him about where he ought to go to high school. Roy asked her where she had been, she had been gone so long, and she said that she had gone to the University of Ohio where she had got her Ph.D. in Education. Roy didn't know what to make of that and neither did anybody else. Everybody in his family figured that she was out to become superintendent of the county schools, but when September came, Hilda was right back at Yellowhawk teaching her fourth graders. Roy's sister Caroline, who was married to Paul Lee and had a baby, said that Hilda had gone a little queer in the head after spending so much time and money going to school, and look what it had got her. She had only gone away because Iris McQuarter had gotten married, and when she came back she found out that Ethel had died and there wasn't any baby after all. So, according to my sister Caroline, all that education hadn't gotten her what she wanted after all, since what she wanted was a man, namely Iris McQuarter.

Roy stayed out of it and listened to them talk, but he was curious about what Hilda would do next. She had all those degrees and she was still living alone out on her farm in Bright April Valley and teaching the fourth grade at Yellowhawk. Nobody bothered her, but nobody paid much attention to her, either. She was a loner, and she had set herself up to be a spinster. It looked to Roy like it was too late for anyone at all to look twice at Horsey Hilda. And I didn't see why Hilda would want to look twice at Iris McQuarter, who was stoop shouldered and sadder every day because of having lost his wife and baby. The only thing Iris had left was his coaching, and his team kept on losing because he couldn't compete with the big boys that manned the county teams.

When it was found out what Hilda intended to do, everyone was so shocked that Roy thought the whole town was going to drop dead right there in the square. Hilda came driving into town one Saturday in her Ford sedan with banners draped all over the car and a big flag flying on the aerial. She had a cardboard megaphone in the front seat beside her and as she came through the main part of town she rolled down her window and yelled as she drove, "Women Unite. The Day of Reckoning Has Come. Women for Better Lives and Better Things." Old Hilda Redfern was going to run the Women's Liberation Movement single handed. She parked her Ford in front of the courthouse and walked into the center of the square, carrying some homemade picket signs and her cardboard megaphone. "Let's go, ladies," she said. "Let's make our own place in the world. It's time for us to stand up and be heard."

People started gathering on the square, not up close to Hilda, just in little circles around the courthouse. They would stand together like they were talking to each other and watch Hilda out of the corner of their eyes. The women stood around with their children and smiled like they were exchanging recipes or gossip. But Roy could tell by the way they kept their children right beside them and didn't let them go darting off so they would have to go after them that they wanted to hear what Hilda had to say. People in the drugstore and the grocery store stopped their work and stood along the window, watching Hilda as she ranted and raved and yelled through her microphone, showing picket signs, pointing to her car, thumping herself on the chest. She talked about Education, Freedom, Better Jobs and Higher Pay. Then she yelled things about bed and babies, and that's all men want, and the preacher from the First Baptist Church started making his way through the crowd to get to her.

Well, by the time the preacher had got there, she must have taken him on, too, because he sort of shrunk back into the crowd where his wife was standing with their five children. He must of tried to get his wife to go home, because she shook him off and remained firm in the courthouse square, listening to Hilda and shaking her head.

Roy didn't know how long Hilda would of gone on, but a rain came up and some people said it was sent by God, but a rain of locusts would have been better to stop that woman. But the rain didn't stop Hilda because that night most of the town women left their husbands at home to mind the children and went to Hilda's house on the farm in Bright April Valley to see what was up. Roy's sister Caroline went, too, and she came back and told him what had happened. It seemed that old Hilda was starting up some sort of free university at her place. She said that the women had had enough 4-H and extension service, they needn't spend their time learning to quilt and can anymore. She said they ought to take advantage of TV dinners and nursery schools and throw out their brooms for vacuum cleaners which they would take turns running with the men. She said it was menial to expect a woman to do house work all day long—that was as bad as the way the colored people were treated in the south and look what was happening there. She got Caroline and her friend Patricia Williams to start a nursery school at their homes, one in the morning, one in the afternoon, to give the women more freedom. And then, she said that the women ought to do something to reawaken and vitalize their minds. So she was setting up a free university at her place, which meant they were to come and study and learn. Anybody could teach anything she was qualified to teach, so long as it didn't have to do with running the house or taking care of the children. The women liked the idea; they all said they'd be there the next evening, whether their husbands liked it or not.

Well, the free university lasted almost a month and it almost broke up Roy's sister Caroline's marriage. Her husband Paul said that if he had to stay home and take care of the baby one more night there wouldn't be any more babies to take care of and Caroline said that's right Paul, now you're getting the idea. This sent Paul packing out of the house and back to his mom's, and Caroline couldn't go to the free university that night because she didn't have any place to leave the baby, and when she came looking for Roy, he hid out so that she couldn't find him.

A few things like that happened to the other women, so Caroline said, but more likely than not, the men were glad to stay at home which was what they did anyway and now, without their wives, they could watch their favorite programs on TV and swig some beer in peace. They didn't realize the danger of Hilda Redfern (Horsey Hilda was now known to some as Freedom's Nag) and her free-school and free-the-women movement.

But then Hilda got her picture in the paper and a big write-up, "Women's Liberation Comes to Eastern Kentucky." This article went by AP to all the big newspapers in Kentucky, and there was a flood of photographers and writers on the square on Saturday mornings. This brought the women out in droves, and no one did any shopping any more, so Roy could stand at the windows in the grocery store and watch the show going on across the street. Hilda was all fired up and talking away about the Mountain Woman, the Pioneer Wife, the I don't know what all. She did a good job and you could almost see the women ready to throw in their rolling pins for good. But then Hilda changed tactics. After she got the photographers and writers there, she started talking about how the real purpose of her free university was to get more women ready and able to teach school as qualified, educated, and intelligent teachers. She said that the county schools would soon be so overstocked with these qualified and intelligent teachers that they would have to send them over to Independent. That must of been what did it. You could just see the superintendent of Independent having a heart attack on the square. Hilda went on cutting Independent, and what she said got written up and published across the country. So the teachers at Independent had a meeting and decided that something had to be done to stop Hilda before it was too late.

That's when Iris McQuarter got pulled into the picture. Iris was just moping along, talking to his friends on the Saturday square or coaching his basketball team at Independent and teaching a little Kentucky history on the side, when somebody was needed to fill in. He was more stoop shouldered and sadder than ever; he didn't seem to care where he was or what he was doing. So the teachers decided to fix him up with Hilda. He didn't want to do it, he said she wouldn't have any part of a man, but they said, "Don't be silly, Iris, this is the only way to shut her up, don't you know that this is exactly what she wants and why she's doing it?" Iris didn't believe them at all, but then he really didn't care any more and it didn't matter if Hilda was County or not, so he said all right, he would give it a try. He said he had known Hilda all his life and they had always been sort of friends, so maybe she wouldn't consider it an insult if he asked her out with him.

So Iris asked Hilda to go with him to the movies and old Hilda dropped her courses at the free university like a hot brick and said she would be back later, the girls could carry on by themselves. She and Iris went out in Iris' green Malibu and Hilda didn't come in until one o'clock in the morning. After that she lay low and didn't hold any more classes or speeches for a week, but Iris didn't call her back so she started up again. Then Independent rallied and told Iris that he just had to do something about this. There was another story in the paper and something had to be done to shut Hilda up for good.

Roy could hear them arguing about it as he stacked and re-stacked the soup cans. The principal and his secretary caught Iris one afternoon as he was doing his grocery shopping—he never bought anything but canned soups and spaghetti—and told him that he had to come across or that was it.

"I'm not saying that I'll fire you, Iris," the principal said. "I know that would be unconstitutional. But I just might not renew your contract."

Iris shrugged his shoulders and gazed across the top of the paper napkins. "I don't know, Elmer," he said. "Why me?"

"Because she likes you, Iris," Betty Blanchard said, flashing her big red-lipped smile and fluttering her mascaraed eye lashes. "Because she'll do anything for you, even be quiet."

"Come on, Iris," Elmer Carter said. "Come on. It won't be so bad. You could even use a woman to look after you. Clean the house, cook your meals, take care of your clothes."

Iris sighed, remembering that he had tried it all once before.

"Come on, Iris," Betty Blanchard waved her secretary's hands in his face. "Come on, for us all."

"She's not going to look after me," Iris said. "You've heard the kind of things she's been saying."

"Now, Iris, that's a bluff," Betty cooed. "That's all a bluff. She's just doing it to catch you. I know, we all know, that's what's behind all this freedom and liberation. Ask any woman what she wants her freedom for and she'll tell you it's to catch a man."

"I'll think about it," Iris promised, loading in more split-pea soup.

Iris must have thought it over because when Roy tried to catch him at the checkout counter next week to ask him what he thought Roy's chances were of playing basketball on the A team at Independent, Roy said he'd have to see me about it later, he was busy. Now this was the first real sign Roy had that something was up, because usually Iris McQuarter was so hot to get his hands on anybody who could tell what a basketball looked like, that he would drop whatever he was doing to get that boy in training right away.

There were two weeks left until school started and once again Hilda Redfern disappeared. Only this time no one saw anything of Iris McQuarter either. Roy sort of missed the excitement of watching Hilda at work on Saturday afternoons in the square. People still milled around and women stood in little huddles waiting for their leader, but she didn't come. Everything was quiet, and the only thing that reminded them all that Hilda had been there thundering for women's freedom was the rain that came up in early afternoon and scattered the crowds.

Then the day before school started Roy was working full time in the grocery, although it was a Monday, when he saw Iris McQuarter's green Malibu pull up by the square. The car was all decorated with tin cans and crepe paper and had been written over on the windows. Happy Honeymoon, it said. Just Married. Tonight's the Night. Hilda got out of the car and marched proudly into the grocery store. "Hello there, Roy," she said.

"Hello, Miss Redfern."

"Well, Roy, it's Mrs. McQuarter now."

"Oh," Roy said. "I see."

Hilda went down the aisles with her cart throwing in cans of this and that, buying just about everything she had ever wanted, it seemed. She didn't use a list this time and she didn't keep her eye cocked on Iris McQuarter who was standing across the street talking to the men in the square.

"Will you be going back to teaching, Mrs. McQuarter?" Roy asked old Hilda as she checked out and told the cashier girl, "Charge it to Iris, please."

"Oh, yes," Hilda said. "I certainly will, Roy. Tomorrow morning."

"Same place, Mrs. McQuarter?"

"Back to my fourth graders."

"And Coach?"

"He'll be back at Independent," Hilda said. "You want me to ask him something?"

"Would you ask him what my chances are of getting on the team? You remember, the basketball team?"

Hilda looked Roy over and gave him a wink. "Didn't you say you're Iris' cousin?" she said.

"Yes, I'm his third cousin."

"That makes you my cousin, too, then Roy."

"Yes, I guess so."

"And that makes your chances awfully good."

"Mrs. McQuarter," Roy said, as old Hilda headed out to the car, letting him push the cart behind her.

"Yes, Roy?" Hilda cocked her head to one side and looked across the street at Iris and smiled. Then she cocked her head to the other side and looked at Roy and smiled again.

"Nothing," he said.

X

"Another new teacher, Hob?" Bill asked his brother Hobie Stone as they stood at the bridge and waited for the schoolbus.

"Yep."

"This your sixth?"

"Yep."

"Six since September! What a record!"

Hobie looked uneasily at the January frozen ground. He knew from the signs that a thaw was due. If hard rains came too, the creeks would rise and the schoolbus couldn't get up Dummit Road. Then Hobie would miss school and break his perfect-attendance record. Worse than that, the new teacher probably wouldn't understand about the creeks rising and she'd mark him absent. Then he wouldn't get the certificate for perfect attendance.

There was an unwritten rule at Yellowhawk that if the schoolbus couldn't get to you, you wouldn't be marked absent. Mr. Jenkins had made the rule and he said it was fair, but not everybody agreed with him. Zania France didn't and she had told Mr. Jenkins to his face that his rule was falsification of the Lord's word and she wouldn't allow it.

Even Hobie's mom said the rule wasn't right. She said you could only be in one place at a time and you couldn't be in one place if you were really in another, so why want to say so? Hobie's mom understood a lot of things about her boys, but she just didn't understand why a piece of paper that said perfect attendance should be so important, and Hobie didn't know how to explain to her that he liked to see his name written down like it was something special.

"Maybe she's right, though," Hobie thought, as he dug one

broganed toe into the ground. "Maybe she's right. No use gettin' a paper that says I been there if I haven't."

On the schoolbus, he sat with Jamie Carter and checked over his arithmetic problems, while he wondered what this new teacher would be like.

Miss Mary Savage was tall and plump. She must have been twice Loretta's size. She had brown hair, too, and pale blue eyes, speckled, like a bird's egg.

Hobie liked her, right away, even though he had decided not to like any more of those teachers. They came and stayed awhile and confused him by telling him different from what the teacher before had told him. They either lowered his marks or raised them so that his mom worried about the way he was gaining or falling off in his work.

"You gotta stick with it all the time, Hobie," she would tell him. "You can't learn nothin' if you just piddle with it now and then. You got to stick with it."

Hobie never argued with his mom or tried to explain about all the teachers who came and went. His mom would only worry about him, and she had enough to worry about these days with a new baby on her hands and Hobie's dad never at home when she needed him. So Hobie didn't say anything about his new teacher Miss Mary Savage or how he liked her or why. But he did like Mary Savage. He liked the way she wrote her name up high on the blackboard, where they could all see it. Hobie found it hard to remember names, and he liked to be able to look up and see who his teacher was in case he forgot. Before the day was over, he even wrote her name in the back of his spelling book, because he always kept the spelling book with him.

Miss Savage was new at teaching. She didn't know how to take up the lunch money or milk money so Tibbie Heineman had to help her. This suited Tibbie fine. She was efficient and she'd helped all the other teachers out. She kept her chair right by the teacher's desk. She could always guess how many would want a hot lunch, and how many had brought their own, and how many wouldn't be eating, so she could tell the new teacher what to do and how to do it. She knew about how to order extra milk and she told Miss Savage to be sure and keep some change for the candy that was sold at noon. Miss Savage smiled and followed Tibbie's suggestions. At first she didn't understand why it was so important to the children to know what was for lunch. Then Tibbie explained that the school lunch was the one big meal a day for most of them, except Kenny Bledsoe who never had any money and was too proud to take a free meal. Kenny stayed in his homeroom during lunchtime and kept his head on his desk. Tibbie told Miss Savage not to say anything to him because it would only hurt his feelings and make him cry.

One thing Hobie and Loretta and Tibbie all liked about Miss Savage was the way she dressed. Their last teacher, Mrs. Morton, had worn only black dresses or black skirts and sweaters. She never put any rouge on her sallow cheeks, and she kept her hair tight and snug in a little knot on the top of her head. But Miss Savage had on a long-sleeved blouse that was covered with red apples with long green stems and leaves, and a dark-green skirt. Tibbie told her girl friends at recess that the blouse had seventeen apples on it. "There might be a couple more under the sleeves," she said. "I couldn't see there too well."

Miss Savage's first week with 7B went well. She learned most of the students' names the first day, and by the second day she could tell them apart even if they were out of their seats.

It was the girls who rode the early bus and got to school at seven thirty, who started straightening up in the room. Then the boys who came in on the seven forty-five would move the seats in line, and dust off the board. Pencils were kept sharpened, the chalk tray wiped out, and Miss Savage's desk as neat as a pin. Since there weren't any flowers in bloom yet, the Hall girl brought in some frozen cattails she'd found by the side of the pond on her way to school. She put them by the radiator until they thawed out. Then Mike Patton brought a jar from the janitor's furnace room, and they put the cattails in it. Tibbie said that the room was finally beginning to look good.

When Miss Savage came in on the Monday of the second week, clutching an armload of children's books, an old globe, crayons and wallpaper, the class relaxed.

"I guess she's going to stay," Catherine Sizemore whispered to her sister Loretta.

"We didn't scare her off after all."

"There's nothing wrong with us," Tibbie insisted. "I told you all that. We're just supposed to be retarded. That's why we're not in Miss Madigan's room. But there's nothing wrong with us."

"These books are from my home," Miss Savage said. "I read them when I was in the seventh grade, and you can, too, if you try."

She let the boys and girls in her "A" Reading Group each choose a book, while she wrote down the student's name and the name of the book on the little file cards she kept in her desk. Then she asked Tibbie and Catherine Sizemore to fasten the wallpaper, creamy side up, to the bulletin board. She gave them blue tacks to hold the paper. She asked Mike Patton to arrange the crayons in a box on the bookshelf.

The class had never colored or drawn much besides left-over hectographed pictures, which they were sometimes given by the second- and third-grade teachers. But now Miss Savage said they were to make a long picture on her roll of wallpaper.

"Draw whatever you like," she said. "Draw something you know well."

Hobie Stone drew a lumpy picture of his hound dog, Jake. He drew Jake cuddled against the logs stacked on his back porch. One of Jake's ears was back behind a rough, round stick of wood. "To keep warm," Hobie said. "Jake has a cold ear." Everyone laughed.

Miss Savage nodded and Hobie drew more—the steep muddy hill his house was perched on, and the clothes line he and Bill had put up. He even made tiny sketches of his mom hanging clothes. He was a little embarrassed to draw his mom, though, so he made her littler than Jake.

Miss Savage said this was all right. She called it perspective. She said when things were scattered over a distance, they weren't all the same size.

Tibbie drew pretty dresses and colored them loud, happy colors; Jamie Carter made a large picture of a tractor, showing its wheels, seat, steering wheel; he sketched a special blade or two to one side of it. "I help my dad in the summer and fall," he explained.

Everyone in the class drew something, even Tullie Cameron. And everybody thought that Miss Savage was fine. She went outdoors at noon and recess and watched the seventh grade play Red Rover. Then when the boys went off together to play tag and the girls huddled in a group for drop-the-handkerchief, Miss Savage would stand in the middle, so she could make sure the boys didn't fall in the creek or climb a tree or slip under the fence and take out across the field. But most of all she liked watching Tibbie Heineman drop the handkerchief behind Loretta, and Loretta taking out after her, her long legs and arms flailing the wind and her brownish-yellow hair flopping up and down.

Hobie Stone began to take more books home. He had always taken his spelling book, because Bill would give him out his words in the evening. And if his dad came home, and he and his mom didn't get along well, Hobie could crawl off into his bedroom and study. But now Hobie took along his literature book. He read each story a day ahead. And he took his geography book and history book, too. He did his homework neatly, and tried not to wrinkle his papers as he dog-eared them together and laid them in his books.

Hobie was a pretty good student for 7B. He made B's in almost everything but arithmetic. He had always made A's in arithmetic because he was good with figures. One thing all of his six teachers had agreed on, was that Hobie Stone was fast and good in arithmetic. He could out-figure any of his classmates. It didn't even take him any time to do the reading problems, although he made a fuss about them. He generally made the fuss because he wanted his classmates to think the work was hard for him, too. He didn't want them to think he was smart and get jealous.

So it was Hobie Stone who noticed that Miss Savage wasn't very good in math. She always carried the seventh-grade arithmetic book with her to school in the morning, along with a little notebook of problems she had worked out the night before. When she sent the class to the board, she sat in an armchair in the back of the room and worked along with them. Sometimes when Hobie had finished and turned to have her check his work, he noticed that she had a funny look on her face and was re-checking the problems in her notebook. So he began to spend a little more time at the board and pretend that the problems were more difficult.

Hobie and all the seventh graders knew that Miss Savage never taught school before. And, because they liked her, they were gentler with her and didn't try to get her out of humor the way they had done sometimes before, like when Tibbie Heineman and Virgil Miller had jumped off the lockers and cawed like crows, scaring Mrs. Morton to death. The class decided not to do anything like that to Mary Savage because they wanted her to stay.

Everybody knew that Miss Savage wasn't out of college yet. They didn't know how much schooling she had had, or where she had got it, but it didn't matter. What counted was that at last they had a permanent teacher, even if maybe their teacher hadn't gone to school as much as some of the others. But Hobie began to wonder just how much math Miss Savage had had. The seventh grade always did their problems right before lunch. When the girl from the cafeteria came to call them early, Miss Savage smiled happily. After lunch, when they were eating their candy bars, she would read them a story. Then they would have the rest of their math period just to work on homework or finish their seat work. Miss Savage would answer their questions as best she could. Or, if she couldn't answer them, she would tell them to ask Hobie Stone.

Hobie was proud, but he didn't take it the wrong way. He never bragged, and he studied more so that he could show his classmates how to do the problems and keep on helping Miss Savage out.

Miss Savage had an Arithmetic Contest. She made Hobie captain of the *Blues,* and Loretta of the *Reds.* She promised a party for the winner. She would buy everyone ice cream, she said, but the losers would serve it and clean up.

So Hobie Stone worked hard on his math. He studied in the evenings and in the mornings after he had milked and had breakfast and gone off to wait for the bus. He studied on his ride to school, and every spare minute he could.

The contest was over the last week of school and the *Blues* won. They had 654 points, and the *Reds* only had 489. Miss Savage said both teams had done well. She wondered who would have won if Hobie Stone hadn't been on either team. Hobie could have been a team of his own, and he still would have won.

"That boy has done more to raise arithmetic grades!" she told the principal. "He has worked with the students as much as I'd let him. I wish there were something we could do—"

Mr. Jenkins looked at Miss Savage. "Hobie likes you," he said. "He'd do anything he could to help you. And he is good in arithmetic, I'll give him credit for that. He's one of the best arithmetic students we have here."

"He's worked so hard."

"Yes. And there is something we can do for him."

"What's that?"

"We can enter him in the county fair's scholastic contest," Mr. Jenkins said. "We'll have Hobie Stone represent Yellowhawk Elementary's seventh grade in arithmetic."

Miss Savage smiled. "He'll win," she said.

"I know he will," Mr. Jenkins agreed.

The last of May was beautiful. There were wild flowers to bring to school and put in the green glass vases Miss Savage had brought from home. Birds' nests brought in by the students were perched on the rafters, and tadpoles swam in a glass bowl. The winter roll of wallpaper had been taken down and replaced with a new, green paper that was covered with pictures of spring things: flowers, creek banks, moss, sunlight, wind puffing at the ankles of children running through the grass.

The days were so warm that the windows were opened in the afternoons. Miss Savage read stories about summer vacations and played a record of a man reading poems about spring. There was music on the record that sounded like a little brook flowing over its rocks and sticks. When Tibbie Heineman said the music sounded like a brook, and the girls all laughed, Miss Savage smiled at Tibbie and explained that this was some famous music that was meant to sound like water. This made Tibbie sit very still in her little chair and listen intently. She didn't understand the poetry, but the sound of the water made her want to run and play in the grass. She was glad school would soon be out.

Mr. Jenkins held a program in the gym on the last Friday. He gave a short speech about everyone having a nice summer and coming back in September all ready to start studying again. Then he had everyone clap for the eighth graders who would be going on to high school. After that he presented certificates for perfect attendance and called out the honor roll.

The certificates had to be taken to the first-, second-, and third-grade students, who were too little to find their way up to the stage and back to their seats again. But everyone else whose name was called marched proudly to the stage and waited to be told Perfect Attendance or Honor Roll.

Hobie Stone was surprised to hear his name called. He, Jamie Carter, and Tibbie Hieneman were all given perfect-attendance papers. "I told you she wouldn't mark us absent," Tibbie hissed to them as they hurried to the stage. "It wasn't our fault the bus didn't run when the creeks were high."

"I guess not," Hobie thought. But for some reason the award wasn't too important for him. When he felt the paper in his hand, he wondered what his mom would think. She would be proud, Hobie knew. But she would be prouder of the report card he would take home, too. This last six weeks, he had made the honor roll.

"I have only one thing more to say," Mr. Jenkins said, when everyone had got back to his seat. "I want to tell you who will be representing Yellowhawk Elementary at the county fair scholastic contests next September."

Hobie Stone didn't believe it when he heard his name called. He had been chosen to go to town and take a test and win a prize! What would his mom think? Not even Bill had ever been asked to be in a contest. Hobie was the only one from his family. Now he knew why the perfect-attendance paper wasn't as important to him as he had thought it would be. Why, it didn't really mean anything. It only said that he had been at Yellowhawk every day, even though he hadn't. Even though, as Tibbie said, it hadn't been his fault—still, he hadn't been there. But this being asked to go to the fair—this was another thing! This showed that when he had been at Yellowhawk, he had studied hard and learned. This was what mattered.

"Don't forget everything you know over the summer," Mr. Jenkins said to Hobie as he waited in line for his bus. "I want you to take first place in September."

"I will," Hobie said. "I'll win."

He wondered where Miss Savage would be then. Probably back at school herself. But she would see the county paper with his name in it and she would be very proud.

❧ XI ❧

As soon as Christmas was over in the county, the girls in the drugstore cleared away the unsold ribbon and paper and cards and set up their valentine displays. It wasn't much of a job, but the girls always took their time about it, because no one was in much of a hurry about buying valentines. And that was the funny thing, considering how many valentines went and came there in the county. Janie knew all about it, though, because she listened to the talk at home, and she knew that everybody went out of town to buy valentines, so nobody would know what they'd bought, and then brought them home and wrote on them, and took them back out of town to mail, so the postmark wouldn't be Short Junction.

Once when she came into the living room, Evie was sitting all propped on the couch with a book in her lap, but she wasn't reading at all, because she had the book upside down and a pencil in her hand.

"What are you doing, Evie?" Janie said. "Writing your valentines?" And you should have seen her face. She was mad. She said, "Janie, don't you ever say that to me! Do you want to get me in trouble, or something?"

Well, Janie had only said it for a joke, she didn't have any idea that her sister was really writing valentines, Evie only being fifteen and all, and so she said, no, she didn't want to get anybody in any trouble, she just hadn't known that Evie had a boy friend, who was he, Pat's big brother Jack or the little one, Joey? Evie looked like she was going to hit her sister, and she said, "No, stupid, I haven't got a boy friend, and besides, if I did, it wouldn't be them, I wouldn't be caught dead with either one of those Holbrook boys."

Janie would have left the room, but she got the idea that Evie sort of wanted to tell what she was doing, so she went along with her, and said, "Well, Evie, who's it to?"

"Promise you won't tell?"

"Of course I won't tell. You know I'm too big for that. Besides, who would I tell, anyway?"

"Mom or Dad."

"Oh, I wouldn't tell them," Janie said. "Come on, who's it to?" she was getting tired of the game, and Evie had made her mad, saying she was still a tattletale. No eleven-year-old girl is going to tell things any more.

"It's to Possum Arthur."

"Who?"

"Possum Arthur. Porter Arthur," Evie giggled.

"Mr. Arthur?" Janie almost shouted. "The principal?"

"For the Lord's sakes, put your voice down," Evie snapped. "Yes, that's what I said: Mr. Arthur."

"Evie, you're out of your mind. Why on earth would you want to send him a valentine?"

"Oh, it's not from me," Evie said. "It's from Bea."

Janie didn't understand, but she knew she'd gotten under Evie's skin, and Evie was determined to tell her, even if she didn't want to know.

"Bea?"

"Look, Janie," Evie said. "Everybody knows Porter Arthur is crazy for Bea, and she won't even look at him. Well, I'm going to fix it up for them. I'm going to send him all these valentines, and make them look like they're coming from her. And then I'll send her a couple, later on, like they're from him. And that'll fix them up and get them together."

Evie looked like she always looked when she thought she had a good idea.

"Are you really going to do it?" was all Janie could think of to say.

"Sure I am. I've already sent two."

"Where did you get them?" Janie asked her.

"At the drugstore," she said. "Nobody ever buys them there, and no one would pay any attention to me getting them, anyway."

"Where are you mailing them from?"

"The post office."

"Here in town?"

"Sure," she said. "I want it to look authentic."

Janie shook her head. "I don't know, Evie," she said. "It doesn't sound right."

"Why not?"

"Mr. Arthur's your principal," Janie said. "And besides, I don't think Bea likes him at all."

"She used to," Evie said. "I know. I heard Mom and Dad talking about it one night. They said she used to be stuck on him."

"I don't believe it. He's too old. Besides, he's fat and bald."

"He just lost his hair a couple of years ago. After Bea quit going out with him. That's when he put on the weight, too. I've heard Mom say that if he had a wife to look after him, he'd be a nice-looking man, still."

"He's too old," Janie repeated.

"He's not much older than Bea," Evie said.

"He must be forty at least."

"Well, what's wrong with that? You think that people don't like each other any more, just because they're over thirty or something?"

"I don't guess so."

"Do you want to see it?" Evie asked then. "The valentine?"

Janie shook her head.

"Well, why not?"

"It just doesn't seem right to me."

"Oh, come on and look."

Evie opened up the book, and Janie saw a big red heart with lots of lace and cupids holding their bows and arrows. Evie had written in under the printed message, "I think of you all the time. I'm sorry for what happened. Let's try again."

"Oh, Evie," Janie said.

"You like it?"

"I don't know," Janie said. But she was impressed, and Evie could tell.

"Do you think he'll know the handwriting?"

"No," Janie said. "I wouldn't even know it was yours, if I hadn't seen you do it."

"Does it look familiar to you?"

"No."

"Not at all?"

"No."

"Of course it does. It has to. See what I've got here?" she pulled a sheet of paper out of the book. "A letter from Bea to Mom. I'm copying her writing."

Janie looked at the letter, one sent to Mom last summer when Bea was on vacation with her sister down at the lake. Then she looked at Evie's valentine, and she knew they were all in for something. The writing on it was just too close to be true. Janie got really scared then, because she thought that Evie would turn out to be a forger or something, and give the family a bad name, and upset Mom for the rest of her life.

She started to go outside and think about it all.

"Wait for me and walk me to the post office," Evie said. "I'm almost through, and we'll get this one in the mail."

Janie didn't want to do it, but she knew that if she backed out, she'd never hear the end of it. Evie would tease her and since Janie wouldn't be able to say why, Evie never would stop unless Janie gave her something that she wanted, like her new yellow sweater. So she went on out to the kitchen and told Mom that they were going to walk downtown, but they'd be back soon. Mom said all right. She gave Janie some money and asked her to stop in at the grocery for some things she'd forgotten to get.

It took Evie fifteen or twenty minutes to get the envelope to suit her, and then they put on their coats and started down Main Street. They didn't talk about the valentine all the way, not even when Evie bought the stamp and dropped it in the box outside the post office. She was so cool about it all that Janie had to admire her for it, and once it was done, she started wondering just what would happen to Bea and Mr. Arthur.

Janie liked Mr. Arthur a lot; she thought he was a real good principal, even if people did say he kept a sloppy school and let his teachers spend too much time in the lounge, drinking coffee and smoking. And Janie thought Bea was all right, too, even though she was a little funny in her ways and didn't come around to the house much like she used to. Janie guessed it was true what Mom had said to Dad one night, when they thought no one was listening, that Bea's one marriage had almost done her in, what with all the drinking Chuck did and him not able to keep a steady job so that Bea had to support him, and then that one time when he'd sold all her antiques and she had to go around to the second-hand stores and buy them back. She had been crying real hard that day they saw her in the car with her mother and sister, and when Mom had stopped by to say hello, Aunt Hattie, Bea's mother, had said that Mrs. Riley was charging her too much to buy the lamp back and Bea wasn't going to pay it, and Bea had her lips pressed together real tight and was looking straight ahead of her. Mom had sent Janie on to the store, but Janie looked back through the windows and saw Mom going into the store together with Bea, and when they came back out Bea had the lamp in her arms, and Mom looked mad, too.

Janie never did know anything about Bea and Mr. Arthur, she had just guessed it was all over for Bea, like Mom and Dad had said, but the more she thought about it, the more she did remember seeing them sitting together a couple of times at basketball games, and then Mr. Arthur had started coming to church and sitting in the pew behind them, and all the family had been real nice to him and said, "Hello, Porter, nice to see you here," and they had invited him home a couple of times for Sunday dinner. But all that was a couple of years ago, before Evie had graduated from Yellowhawk and gone on to high school.

When they went into the grocery, Evie hit Janie in the stomach with her elbow, and when Janie looked up, there was Bea, standing in front of the counter marked "Toiletries." She didn't see them, and Janie was about to say something but Evie gave her a hard look and they went over behind the vegetables and watched Bea from there, even though Janie didn't like it, it looked too much like spying. Bea took down a card of hair rollers and a jar of face cream, real quick-like, and dropped them in her cart. Then she went on to buy some bread, and Evie turned around and said, "Why, hi, Bea."

Bea looked sort of funny. She took another loaf of bread and put it over the hair rollers and said, "Hello, there, Evie. Hi, Janie. What are you doing here?"

"Shopping for Mom," Evie said. "We'd better hurry, too. She's waiting for us."

"I'll give you a ride," Bea said. "I just have to stop in the drugstore first."

"No, that's all right, we want to walk." Evie grabbed Janie and pushed her on toward the checkout counter.

"What's wrong with you?" Janie said, when they were out of the grocery. "And what's wrong with riding with Bea? She's got a nice car."

"Possum Arthur's in the drugstore," Evie said, "and I didn't want Bea to feel rushed. Come on, now."

They started up the street and about fifteen minutes later Bea pulled up beside them and said, "Come on, girls, get in." Janie didn't wait for Evie to say no this time. She opened the door and got up in the front seat of Bea's new Chevrolet. Evie came behind her. Bea was sort of excited. She had trouble getting the car started and there were bright pink spots on her cheeks. When they got to the house, Bea got out first, and said, "I want to see your mother for a minute."

Mom was real pleased that Bea had come by. She poured her a cup of coffee and said, "Sit down."

Bea nodded and didn't say, "I've only got a minute," like she had been doing before.

She seemed to be wanting to say something, and Janie thought it must be because of her and Evie hanging around that Bea didn't know quite what to do.

Finally Janie couldn't stick it out any longer—watching Bea so miserable made her nervous—so she went on up to her room to do her homework, and Evie came, too. Bea got up and closed the kitchen door, but the girls could hear her saying to Mom, ". . . what's got in to him, but . . .," and then the door slammed and her voice trailed off.

Bea stayed for forty-five minutes and supper was late that night. Mom looked funny when they all sat down to eat and nobody had much to say. When they were through, Mom said,

"Now you girls run along. I want to talk to your father." Evie and Janie went to their room and Janie noticed it took Evie a long time to settle down and start to work. I guess she's getting worried about what she'd done, Janie thought. But then she knew Evie and she knew that once Evie had started a thing, she would see it through. Now Evie had got it in her head to send these valentines, and unless she got caught, she'd keep it up. And Janie wasn't going to be the one to tell on her.

The next Sunday, Mr. Arthur was back in church, back in the pew behind them, and it wasn't hard to watch Bea's face when she heard him come in, say hello to everyone, and sit down. But Bea didn't turn around and look at him and she sat real still all through the service and didn't sing very loud. The sermon was on the beauty of love, or something like that, and when Reverend Chester was waving his arms and talking of Love, Janie heard someone in the row behind shifting his feet a lot and clearing his throat. Janie wondered if it was Porter Arthur, and she wondered why they called him Possum Arthur and if Bea knew that he had that nickname.

After church, Mom seemed to make a beeline for the door, and then they all waited around outside, even though it was cold, for Bea to come out. When she did, Mr. Arthur was right behind her, and Mom stepped up and said, "Why, good morning, Bea. Good morning, Mr. Arthur," like she hadn't seen either of them for a long time. They said something to each other and then Mom raised her voice and said, "Why don't you both come home and have dinner with us?" Janie looked at Evie and she thought Evie was going to die. Evie was turning all shades of red, just at the thought of having the high school principal there in the house, and Janie knew she was wondering what the other kids would say when they found out. Evie didn't set herself up to be a teacher's pet and she couldn't stand being teased, but who knows, Janie thought, maybe it will do her a little good, especially after what she's been doing with her valentines.

So Bea and Porter Arthur came to the house, and Janie was surprised at how Mom had things almost ready for dinner, and how there seemed to be enough for the six of them with no trouble at all. At dinner, Dad did most of the talking, and the others just listened. Bea kept her eyes close to her plate, and Porter Arthur didn't seem to know what to say except when Dad asked him if he'd been doing much hunting and he said, "Oh, yes," and told about how good his dogs were. Janie thought Bea would die. She never did take much to killing things, and she had all these bird boxes up around her house and put out food for the squirrels and rabbits. But Bea didn't say anything at all. She just listened, with her eyes down on her plate. Then Mr. Arthur said how he had this deer meat in his freezer, and he'd be glad to bring some by to Mom, if she'd make him some burgoo, which is venison stew, and he'd take some to Bea, too, if she'd like, and Bea said, well, yes, she just might, and turned sort of red, then, and said she'd get up and get the coffee. Porter Arthur shuffled his feet and said, "Oh, excuse me," and Dad said, "That's all right," as he moved his legs, and nobody knew quite what to do while Bea rattled around with the spoons and cups and waited for her face to cool off before she came back to the table.

After that, January seemed to go real quickly and before anybody knew it February was here. Valentine's Day was coming and in Janie's homeroom they were making a valentine box, decorating it with crepe-paper ruffles and construction-paper hearts. It didn't seem too silly, doing it this year, and Janie felt all excited, like something special was going to happen on Valentine's Day.

Evie didn't have much to say. Janie didn't know if she was sending any more valentines or what. She thought Evie must have quit, though, because she was just sitting back and waiting, too, like something was going to happen.

So neither one of them was at all surprised when on Valentine's Day morning at two o'clock, the telephone rang. They both woke up with a start and sat up in bed with the covers pulled around them. The phone kept on ringing, and then they heard Dad stumble down to the kitchen and answer it, and say, "Hello, hello, who is this?" Then he was quiet, just listening, and then he said, "All right, all right." Then he didn't sound sleepy any more; he said, "Who? Where are you? You are? When?" and Janie heard him laugh, as he yelled for Mom. She came down the hall in her bathrobe and slippers and took the phone away from him. Then she started laughing, too. She talked some, but they couldn't hear what she said, and then she gave back the phone to Dad, and he said, "Well, see you soon," and hung up and they went back to bed with their arms around each other's waists.

Evie and Janie didn't go back to sleep until after five, and when Mom called them at seven, it was hard to get up. Downstairs in the kitchen, the coffee was on the stove and Mom was frying bacon and Dad was in there with her. Janie could hear them talking and laughing as she went in.

"Did you hear the phone ring last night?" Mom asked.

Janie nodded and got a glass of orange juice.

"Did you know who it was?"

"No."

"That was Bea and Porter Arthur calling," Mom said, with a big smile. "They drove over into Indiana last night and got married."

Janie didn't know what to say, but she thought Evie was going to drop her coffee cup.

"Got married?" Evie squeaked out finally. "That late at night?"

"Yes, they wanted to wait until Valentine's Day."

"I didn't think Porter Arthur had it in him to be that romantic," Dad said.

"Oh, Jeff," Mom laughed. "Not in front of the girls!"

Dad ate his bacon and eggs, and then he looked up at Mom and said, "You know, Ethel, I think you must have had a hand in all of this. I think you knew something all along. I must say, they really pulled the wool over my eyes."

Mom had a twinkle in her voice when she said, "Oh, now, Jeff, I've had an idea, but I wouldn't say I knew exactly. Except that they have been interested in each other a long time."

"Well, it beats me," Dad said. "I thought that was over two years ago. Never did figure out exactly what happened, but I thought it was over. I don't guess it was, though. Couldn't have been. Weren't they the sly ones?"

"Not sly, Jeff," Mom said. "They were just waiting. They wanted to make sure."

"Just waiting?" Dad snorted. "Well, they almost waited too

long. They're not getting any younger, you know."

"I know, I know," Mom said.

Then she looked up at Janie and Evie. "Hadn't you girls better go out to catch the school bus?" she said. "You're almost late."

"I don't guess," Dad said as they left the room, "there's any need in asking them not to tell. It'll be all over the school in just half an hour, you know."

"Let them talk," Mom said. "The news has to get out some-time."

Janie thought it was some kind of poetic justice for Evie to be the one to tell, as soon as they climbed on the schoolbus, that Mr. Arthur and Bea had gotten married last night. And when she saw her sister running ahead to get on first, she knew that's just what was going to happen. But Janie didn't really care. She had something else on her mind.

If it had worked for Bea, she thought, it just might work for somebody else. When the drugstore put their valentines on sale half-price, she was going to go down and buy up all they had left. She'd say she was getting them for next year, if anybody asked her. And she was going to send them all. It didn't make any difference that Valentine's Day was over. If people started sending them after Christmas, why not keep on sending them until Easter? There were a lot of lonely people around Short Junction, she thought, and it was about time that some of them got together. Just like Bea and Porter Arthur. Yes, the valen-tines were going to fly.

⚜XII⚜

"Damnation," said Mr. Pennywise with a snort, when he saw Alfie Crump's shiny close-cropped head bobbing under the windowsill. "Damnation. Here he comes again." Mr. Pennywise bit hard on the stump of his five-cent cigar.

There was a rap on the door.

"Yes?"

The frosted glass seemed to melt as Alfie Crump came oozing through the black print of the Pennywise & Pennywise Law Offices. He stood, shifting silently from one foot to the other, with a wet, whimpering smile on his bleak face.

"Yes, Alfie? What can I do for you today?"

"I've got troubles, Mr. P."

Mr. Pennywise flinched. He hated to be addressed as Mr. P. "Proper nomenclature," he would mutter for hours after Alfie Crump drifted back down the main street, walking as sluggishly as a rain-soaked leaf bobbing in weak autumn wind.

"Come now, Alfie, everyone has troubles. We just don't let them get the best of us," Mr. Pennywise said, clenching his expensive black fountain pen—a gift from the other Mr. Pennywise, his son Cole, who had just returned to continue his studies at Maysville Junior College. Mr. Pennywise, Senior, proud that his son would soon enter law practice, had gone ahead and added the second Pennywise to the frosted window as proof of his approval and anticipation.

"I should think not, Mr. P."

"Eh, what's that?" Mr. Pennywise said irritably. He was thinking how handsome the black fountain pen was.

"I should think not. Everyone having troubles—how could they? 'Everyone' would be countin' Ida Louise."

"Oh," said Mr. Pennywise. "So that's what it is. You're right, my boy. Not everyone does have that problem, thank goodness." ("Damnation," Mr. Pennywise thought. "If that's all that's troublin' him, why doesn't he get out of here? I've got work to do?" And he dipped the pen carefully into the inkwell, pulling out the metal slide with his thumbnail and counting to three while the pen guzzled in jet black permanent Quink.)

But Alfie was not to be put off.

"I thought you might help me. You might put in a good word for me, so to speak."

Mr. Pennywise looked across his huge polished desk at little Alfie Crump. His irritation changed to dislike. 'A good word for you?' He wanted to say: 'Damnation, boy, what do you expect?'

"You could do it very discreetly," Alfie continued. "You knowin' Ida Louise's family, and all."

'Yes,' Mr. Pennywise thought, 'and I don't intend to sing your idle praises.'

"Naturally, I would do an exchange."

"What's that?"

"An exchange. For your help. I have a service to exchange."

Mr. Pennywise shook his black coat sleeves over his white starched shirt cuffs. He gripped his cigar stump hard between his yellowed teeth. He leaned farther across the polished desk. He was getting interested. What could Alfie Crump do for him? Alfie Crump was a Yellowhawk dropout who clerked at the store on Saturday, made banana splits in the ice-cream shop on Sunday, and sent telegraph signals at the railway station all through the week.

Alfie halfway twisted himself around so Mr. Pennywise couldn't see the expression on his face. His sticky, thin hair glared in the lamp light. Mr. Pennywise noticed a pencil stuck behind his ear, and some labels in his left trousers pocket.

"For puttin' in a good word with Ida Louise's family—you know, sayin' I'm a nice young man, hard workin', industrious—" Alfie raised his head, and Mr. Pennywise saw a smile flicker across his bald features—"I am prepared to render unto you a great and valuable exchange."

"Well, get on with it, get on with it." Mr. Pennywise was

beginning to be irritated by Alfie's sudden spurt of loquacity.

"Perhaps...no, no, I really couldn't presume, Mr. P. Thank you, but excuse me for having troubled you." And Alfie began to ooze back toward the frosted door.

"Well, I never." Mr. Pennywise chewed frantically on his cigar. Here Alfie Crump had interrupted his work, whetted his interest on some half-witted thing or other, and now he was going to just drop the matter and leave him hanging in mid-air.

"Your behavior, Crump, is distasteful," said Mr. Pennywise. "Here, have a cigar and take some advice from an old man. Never start a thing without finishing it. See it through. Get it done. Stick with it, boy. It may be just a trouble now—but if you don't stop it, if you don't lick this trouble at the start, think of what a problem it might grow into...you know how the corn does, Alfie. You're a farmer's boy. Starts from a little seed, and springs right sky-high. Same way with troubles."

"I guess you're right, Mr. Pennywise, sir," he said, without turning around.

Mr. Pennywise put the cigar back in his pocket. "Of course I'm right, boy. Now tell me your trouble."

"Well, I..."

"Come on, boy," Mr. Pennywise was wheedling. "Don't be shy. Speak up."

"Well, sir, I've got a rival."

"A rival?"

"With Ida Louise." Alfie's cheek was working hard. His eyes were sort of popping out of their sockets, rolling back and forth, and his wispy hair, licked back against his shiny hair, seemed almost to stand up stiff from his anger.

"Well, Alfie," Mr. Pennywise said, "that sounds natural to me. Ida Louise is a right pretty girl. Not many girls as pretty as she is, here in town."

"Not any girls," Alfie corrected.

"All right, Alfie. Not any girls," Mr. Pennywise agreed pleasantly. All females looked the same to him, anyway. Almost. "Who is your rival?"

"Well, sir, that involves the service I could do for you. With the other Mr. Pennywise."

"Who?"

"The other Mr. Pennywise. Cole Pennywise, your son."

"Cole?"

"Yes, sir. Mr. Pennywise."

"I'm afraid I don't understand, Alfie."

"Well, sir, you've got plans for your boy, haven't you?"

"Yes, Alfie, I do," Mr. Pennywise said, proudly, stuffing his fat fingers in his lapels and pulling out his collar. "Big plans. My boy is going to be a lawyer. A good lawyer. He's going to get the best education Maysville Junior College can offer. Then, it's Europe for him if he wants it. Or East for more schooling. Then, someday, I'll settle him down here, in a brand-new office, and those words 'Pennywise & Pennywise' will mean something!"

Alfie shrugged uncomfortably. "I doubt that, Mr. P.," he said.

"What's this?" Mr. Pennywise almost dropped his cigar. "What's this?"

"It's just that..." Alfie looked down at the cracked, warped tops of his heavy brogan shoes. He licked his lips and opened his mouth, but he didn't speak. He just closed his mouth and stood there, staring at his feet.

"What's this?" Mr. Pennywise stepped out from the bounds of his big desk. "What do you know about Cole?" he asked. "You'd better tell me, Alfie."

"Well, sir," said Alfie, between his teeth, "I hear that your son has his own ideas—I hear that he has his mind made up to settle down."

"What's this?" Mr. Pennywise repeated.

"With a girl..."

"A girl? Cole? ahahahahaha," Mr. Pennywise made a gritty little noise between his teeth, a little noise that slipped around and out from under his cigar. It sounded like a laugh. "You've got your wires crossed, Alfie. Cole Pennywise never laid eyes upon a female except to offer her a polite good morning or good afternoon. Not my Cole. He's going to travel. To study. To be somebody big here in town."

"That's the rumor, sir," Alfie twitched his lips. "Rumor is he's good as married—meanin' that he's fixin' to," Alfie added.

"Crump," Mr. Pennywise clenched his little fists as hard as

knots and held them down at his sides. "Crump, are you tellin' me the truth? So help me, speak up. I want to know."

Alfie sidled a few steps away from Mr. Pennywise and stood on tiptoe, peering from the window so that all that showed was his profile, with his nervous jaw muscle twitching away.

"Truth, sir."

"Alfie—" Mr. Pennywise was pleading. "Alfie, you can back out. You can say, 'hahah, it was all a joke, Mr. P.' and I'll understand—no trouble..."

"It's truth, sir."

Mr. Pennywise slumped back into his big round chair, knocking aside one of the hand-crocheted arm pads that covered the frayed fabric.

"Who's the girl?"

"Can't tell you, sir."

"Do you know her?"

"Yes, sir."

"Nice girl?"

"Yes, sir."

"Honorable?"

"Oh, yes, sir."

"Good family?"

"Yes, sir."

"How much?"

Alfie didn't answer.

"How much do you want, Alfie?"

Alfie took out a wad of chewing gum and stuck it in his mouth. Taking his time, he masticated the gum from side to side, working it, massaging it, encouraging it. His eyes were working, too, flitting back and forth from the nervous Mr. Pennywise in his too-large chair to the leaves falling from the large oak by the window.

"Not just money," he said, softly. "Just a bargain."

"A bargain?" Mr. Pennywise, too, spoke softly.

"A bargain. An exchange." Alfie shoulders rippled nervously. Mr. Pennywise was aware of the hard muscles beneath Alfie's blue shirt.

"What do you want?"

For a moment, Alfie was silent. Then he turned to Mr. Pennywise. "I'm only Alfie Crump," he said. "Seventh-grade education just because Miss Savage passed me. Dropped out because I had to go to work. Now I'm eighteen years old and I clerk at the store on Saturday afternoons, work in the ice-cream shop on Sunday, and send railroad signals all through the week. When anybody wants an errand done, they call for Alfie. And I do it. But if I had a good job, and a little money in the bank, I could dress up and be somebody. I could wear a suit and a tie and trade the truck in for a good used car. We wouldn't need the pick-up any more, because I wouldn't be hauling garbage to the dump. Then I could go in front doors, instead of crawling around back quiet-like so I could pick up garbage without disturbing anybody.

"A little money in the bank would make me a down payment on a farm where I could make my own living. I could help out my folks and see that my sister goes to high school. We wouldn't need her to help pick tobacco and do chores because we could hire somebody."

Mr. Pennywise was listening.

"A little money in the bank, and a job," Alfie repeated. "Not much of a job to start with." He glanced around Mr. Pennywise's office, staring at the door lettered "Pennywise & Pennywise." "This place needs to be kept tidied up. I'm good at things like that. I'm smarter than you think, Mr. Pennywise. I've learned a lot at the store. I can figure and file and sort and stack. I've learned a little typewritin' at the railroad office. Picked it up by myself. The ice-cream parlor's taught me to deal with people in a friendly manner. I learn fast.

"And I've got friends. Why, before you know it, you'll have more clients than you know what to do with. They'll fill this office—they'll stand in the hall, even on the steps, waitin' for you to help them. I could help! I could tell you their names, their troubles, what they can afford to pay you! Oh, I could help you plenty, Mr. Pennywise."

"What about Cole?" Mr. Pennywise asked hoarsely.

"With a little money in the bank and a good job, I could take care of that, too," Alfie said. "A new suit of clothes, a box of candy, and the Saturday movies talk big to a girl. When you throw in a couple of ice-cream sodas and a hymn-singin' partner for church, you really talk big."

"How can you be sure that would talk big to Cole's girl?" Mr. Pennywise asked.

Alfie looked Mr. Pennywise straight in the eye. "Ida Louise is a sensible girl," he said. "She doesn't really want too much from life...just a little more than she's got now. Besides, I'm sure she'd listen to you, sir, if you was to talk to her."

Mr. Pennywise was thoughtful. He turned himself around, in his big chair, so that he, too, could look at the proud black letters painted on his door. "Pennywise & Pennywise," he murmured.

Alfie said nothing.

Mr. Pennywise clutched his big expensive fountain pen in his balled-up fist. "Seventy-five dollars, in advance," he said, printing the check carefully. "Work here begins at eight o'clock in the morning. Bring your own lunch. You can leave at five if we're done. If not, you stay until we finish. We've got a lot to do—understand?"

"Oh, yes, I understand," Alfie smiled. Taking the check from Mr. Pennywise's outstretched hand, he rolled it between his thumb and index finger, just to see if the paper felt good.

"Well, I'll be going now," he said softly. "I have to hand in my resignations. Do a little shoppin'. Get a good night's sleep. Don't worry—I won't be late, though. I get up with the sun. I'll be here when you come in."

Alfie oozed toward the door. His big hand shot out and grappled with the doorknob. The tip of his brogan shoe moved just a little, and he was standing on the threshold, his cropped head bobbing beneath Pennywise & Pennywise.

"You do that, Alfie," Mr. Pennywise said in a small voice that barely reached from desk to door.

"No, sir, I won't be late my first morning. That would never do."

"No."

"Eight o'clock, Mr. Pennywise."

"Eight o'clock, Alfie."

The door closed, and he was gone.

✥ XIII ✥

When Brad was only a kid and Muffins Royster was still wearing blue jeans under her short, patched cotton skirts to keep her legs warm, Brad used to save his nickels for strawberry soda pop and orange slices. Every Saturday afternoon about three o'clock, Ma took her boy to town to help gather up washings. When they had made the rounds, and packed the dirty clothes neatly in a big cardboard box, Ma went to the Surplus Store to shop for the few things they needed, and Brad was free! Free, for half an hour, to look in the drugstore window at the boxed chocolates, comic books, and playthings. He did this slowly, surveying from left to right the cellophane-protected display. He measured the value of each item, discussing it at length with Muffins, who usually tagged along because her own house was "full of company" and she only "got in the way."

(Whenever Muffins told Ma about the company, Ma would draw her upper lip down tight over her yellow teeth in a straight-line frown that creased all the smiles out of her silky cheeks, and took the nice Saturday blue from her eyes. She would squint and grunt understandingly, then catch Muffins by the back of her scrawny neck and say, "Listen, Muffins, you come see us whenever you want.")

Muffins would advise her friend on his shopping with a solemnity that befitted the spending of their shared pennies. But, as their time ran out and they saw Ma waddling down the street with a brown paper bag tucked under her arm, they would rush in, buy their sodas and orange slices, and begin the long walk home, sipping, munching, and groaning happily under the weight of the cardboard box.

This was also the year Brad became interested in spooks. It

happened after Muffins came to stay with them. ("That Jeze-bel-on-the-Hill," Ma would mutter under her breath. "No fittin' woman to raise a child.") Muffins and Brad often sat on the back porch at night, stringing beans or cracking hoarded nuts, listen-ing to the puff-puffing of the scented winds in the orchard. Muffins would look up at her friend strangely every so often:

"Did you hear that, Brad?" she'd say, her tiny mouth quiver-ing.

"Naw."

"I did. I heard it. It was a cry. It came from the bog."

"Silly bump. There's no bog around here."

"Yes, there is," she would whisper, leaning across the dishpan of soaking clothes. "Under the sycamore trees, at the foot of Hood's Run. I been there when the haunts was out. I've heard 'em screaming. I know what they was saying."

"Muffins, I'll tell Ma on you for fibbin'."

"It's the truth, Brad. One night when we had company—" she looked away—"I slipped out of the house, across the hill. I went to sleep under them trees. When I woke up, I heard that awful screechin'. I saw lights—little silver lights, the size of an acorn, bouncing over the bog."

"What were they?" Brad asked, drawn to her.

"Spirits. Spirits drawing up the dead. They brought the smoke of damned souls from that bog. The smoke was white in the moon, and smelled like lye. It drifted up and nestled in the sycamores. The little lights fizzled, and folded inside it, and I could hear a breathing—like a dead man who rasps out a pocket-ful of air that was caught in his lungs."

Brad sat shaking.

"But that's not all," she smiled secretively. "I know more."

"Tell me," he begged.

"You're too scairty-cat."

"I am not."

She eyed him thoughtfully. "If I tell you—what'll you give me?"

Brad thought. "You can have the feather pillow tonight."

"Got one. Your ma found an old one in the attic. Been airin' it all day."

"The blue marble I found on the street Saturday."

"Won it from you this afternoon."

"All right," he gave in. "What do you want?"

"You got to go with me—to the place I'm goin' to tell you about."

"I dunno."

"There! I told you! Scairty-cat!" she scratched at him with her sharp little nails.

"Ouch," he hollered.

She laughed. "I wouldn't go with you nohow. I wouldn't go with such a baby. I'd be ashamed for them to see me."

"Who?" he asked.

"Never mind," she nodded wisely. "Never mind."

It took Brad's share of the apple pie Ma had set aside for them, and his oldest, most-mended shirt to dress Muffins' cornshuck dolls before she promised to take him "to see them."

They didn't go for a week. Muffins said, mysteriously, that she wasn't ready—she had to wait for the mood—she had to feel the need to visit them. She said they didn't like to be bothered for no reason; they would "spell" her for being worrisome.

Brad grew more anxious as each day passed. Muffins stayed to herself. She made stick playhouses in the soft grass under the walnut tree, decorating them with clumps of moss, baked-mud dishes, and her cornshuck dolls. She avoided him. Ma said she was lonely for her pa, who had gone away a year ago, and just to let her alone. She'd come around.

On Friday night, Muffins laid one small, sunburned hand on Brad's arm, and said softly, "Are you ready, Brad?"

"Yes," he whispered. He knew what she meant.

"Are you sure?"

"Yes."

"Good. We'll go tonight."

After Ma had said her prayers and gone to sleep, they slipped out the back door and down the hollow. Muffins led the way, creeping soundlessly across the slippery grass, shushing Brad each time a twig or leaf crunched beneath his heavy brogan shoes.

She stopped at Millard Liles' cabin at the head of Hood's Run.

"Here's where we've come, Brad," she whispered. Her firm

mouth trembled, and he saw a flicker of something akin to fear in her bright hard eyes.

"I'm not afraid," he lied. "I'm not afraid, Muffins."

She smiled, and raised her hand to unlatch the high gate.

"Muffins, Muffins, will he hurt me? Will the crazy man hurt me?"

"No, Brad."

He believed her. He didn't know why, but he believed her. He shut out the picture of Millard Liles in his old flannel shirt and blue overalls, barefoot even in autumn, chopping wood fiercely, swinging his sharp axe with his powerful arms, striking hard and sure, so that the thick log thumped beneath his foot and the chips flew like hailstones; Millard, shuffling up and down in his garden of wild, weed-infested flowers and broken-colored glass, muttering to himself, shaking his fist at the jagged pale blossoms, cursing them for lacking the beauty they were too sick to show. He closed his ears to Ma's warning: "You stay away from that man, Bradford. He's wicked. Deep down inside, he's wicked, polluted with the mud his filthy house's built in. Akin to the devil, he is."

The door cracked. "Who's there? What'd you want? Why're you botherin' me?"

"It's me, Mr. Liles," Muffins said. She could have been crooning to herself as she wove clover chains—her voice was sing-song, sweet with the innocence of a girl-child who knows only summer and summer things.

Brad heard a strange shuffling, a crackling, and then, "Come in, child. Come and bring your friend. S' that young Bradford?"

"Yes."

"D'you think he is...?"

"Yes."

The door widened. Brad saw the pitch blackness, relieved only by the dim, greasy glow of a half-burned candle. He felt the cold clamminess of that cabin—strange, sinister for an August evening.

They sat in hard-backed chairs, looking at each other across an oilcloth-covered table. Finally Muffins spoke.

"It is time."

Millard Liles sighed. He shifted his weight, and Brad watched his powerful muscles ripple under the dirty flannel shirt. His eyes were huge, sunken in his heavy, leathery cheeks. "Yes," he wheezed.

Millard Liles closed his eyes. Muffins closed hers. As if their sight had been the warmth, Brad felt the air in the cabin growing cooler, stiller, frozen with ruts of silence. His flesh began to crawl. He shook until he had to hold his chair, but he could not close his eyes. He saw them coming, and he could not close his eyes.

The little silver lights began to climb the wall. Slowly at first, then gathering speed, tap-tapping, tap-tapping...beating out a banjo rhythm on the rough, unfinished walls. They breathed heavily, crackling, bursting into flame, circling widly, then fanning out through the cracks.

After the warmth began to come back in the cabin, and the candle threw off a brighter, bluer light, Brad heard Millard Liles say quietly:

"Did they speak to you?"

"Yes."

"Did they tell you?"

"Yes."

"Should he know?"

"Yes." Muffins turned to Brad. Her face was white, crystal cold, drawn and wrinkled like an old woman's. "My ma's going to die."

People said it was on account of her wickedness. She was young—only twenty-some, and a handsome woman, with light-brown hair and hazel-speckled eyes. She had borne three children, two dead, but the third had sprung up like a fresh, wistful flower in the coarse, tainted soil of her existence.

"You're a good woman, to take the child," folks said to Brad's ma. "You're a good woman, Mollie. We'll help you all we can, if you need us."

"She'll be a comfort to you, Mollie. A woman needs a girl-child."

"Your boy needs a sister. It's a lonely life for him, too, in the hollow."

In December, they found Millard Liles. Found him frozen

solid, under the sycamores at the foot of Hood's Run. No one knew why he died, either, unless it was because he was a crazy man. Some said he fooled with the knocking spirits, and they always got a body in the end.

Muffins never said a word about her ma or Millard Liles. She just played with her dolls, and won Brad's marbles, and ate her share of the Saturday orange slices. She gathered soggy leaves when the snows melted, threw sticks in the swollen creek, and raced the frozen winds through the hollow, laughing happily, her brown hair streaming down her neck.

❧ XIV ❧

Corry Alcorn lived in Settlor's Breach, in a white frame house he and his brother Bill had put up one summer when there wasn't any full-time work to be had at the shops, and the plant was so full the foreman wouldn't even make a waiting list. Corry had built two bedrooms, a kitchen, and a living room in the house. Later on, when he was working full time, he dug a cellar in the evenings and put up an outhouse, smokehouse, and a little building to house the Delco.

About the time they got power in the Breach, Bill decided to pull out and go to Ohio, to get in on some of the industry that was filling up the factories with eastern Kentucky's underpaid and unemployed. Bill went, leaving Corry the house and all its fixings, asking for a bed to sleep on when he came back on weekends.

But he didn't come back because he got a good job, seven days a week if he wanted the work, and overtime pay. An Alcorn was known to be a worker, so he stuck to it and drilled out his time in the factory, picking up all the skill at labor that a rough-handed sixth-grade-educated man with a lot of gut and horse sense could take on.

He only had one day without pay cut at Christmas, so Bill Alcorn decided not to go home to Corry and the house snowed in at Settlor's Breach. He went to a church dinner that was given for other people like him, people who had come to Ohio for the work and couldn't get home to be with their own folks for the holiday. People who were lonely and just wanted somebody to talk to, who knew about the things back home.

At the dinner, Bill met a schoolteacher who had been over in Ohio for six months. She was young and green and Bill fell for her pretty helplessness. He walked her back to her boarding house after the prayers that followed dessert. And he promised to see her again.

There wasn't much time for courting in an Alcorn's life. What Bill had going for him was an honest face, hard-working hands, and what Netta Stephenson wrote home to her sister was "good Christian character." He was able to make Netta see that he was worth liking and making a life with, and when he finally found time to ask her, she said yes, she would marry him.

When the letter from Bill came, Corry took it down to Anita Longer to read. Anita was a good friend of his and Corry had a lot of respect for her. She was fifty-five years old but she still walked three miles Monday through Friday to catch the schoolbus and ride to Yellowhawk where she taught her neighbors' kids everything that third graders ought to know.

Anita answered the door of her own green-shingled house with a frown and a glare. She had nothing to do with strangers in the winter time. She had a house to keep up, a job to do, and a twelve-year-old niece to raise. She couldn't be bothered with crazy people who went wandering around this neck of the woods in a storm, apt to be lost or senseless, maybe with a loaded gun or a knife hidden under their belts. But when she saw Corry Alcorn's quiet face and his eyes lit up with some strange excitement, she relaxed her hold on the revolver tucked away under her shawl, swung open the door—although she was usually careful to be sure no friend was being forced in at some crazy man's gunpoint —and let him in.

"Welcome," she said.

Corry stood uncertainly, tramping off snow and melted-down ice on the throw rug Anita put out for him.

"I've a letter," he said at last.

"Well sure enough," Anita cried with a loud laugh. "Come in and I'll read it to you. Who's it from?"

"I can't tell," Corry said. "I've no one who'd write to me, though, unless it's Bill."

Anita Longer took the crumpled envelope from Corry's numb, outstretched hand.

"It is Bill," she said. "See here, Corry—Bill Alcorn—she pointed out the sender's name and return address.

"Uh-huh," Corry said, embarrassed.

"Shall I read it to you?"

"Please, ma'am."

"Dear Corry Alcorn," Anita read. "You must be wondering who I am to write to you this way. My name is Netta Stephenson Alcorn. I am a schoolteacher here in Granger County, and now your brother's wife. He has asked me to write and tell you our good news, that we were married on Valentine's Day, two weeks ago this afternoon. I am looking forward to meeting you, and he to seeing you, when we come down in the spring. Yours sincerely, your new sister, Netta. P. S. Bill asks me to tell you that all goes well here."

Corry sat hunched over in Anita's over-stuffed crochet-covered chair. He looked at the big woman out of round dismal eyes that were filled with tears.

"Bill's married," he sobbed out at last.

"Yes, I reckon so. Sounds like a good woman he's got. She writes a pretty hand."

Corry didn't move a muscle. His face didn't twitch. His feet were still on the hearth, although they were tingling from the heat of the fire.

Anita got up and fetched her sewing basket from the corner. "I'll darn your socks," she said quietly. "They're full of holes."

Corry took them off and handed them over to her.

"You can put these on now," she said. She lifted up the top of the cedar chest that stood against the wall and handed Corry a pair of almost-new heavy wool socks.

"They were Ed's," she said. "He made me promise I'd give his things to someone who needed them."

Corry drew on the warm dry stockings. "Thank you," he said.

"It's all right," Anita smiled. She looked around her to make sure her niece was not up and about the house. When she had satisfied herself that Cam's snore was a true one, she brought out half a bottle of whiskey from her store of third-grade posters, charts, and books, and offered it to Corry.

"I never touch it," he told her.

"Go ahead," she said. "You could use this tonight. It's been a cold walk down and you've had a shock. I'll make you some coffee afterward."

Corry stared at the bottle.

"It was Ed's," she said. "It's never been touched in the four years he's been gone. But I kept it like he said to. I guess he knew there'd be a need for it."

Corry took the bottle and had a stiff drink. Then, his eyes smarting from the strength of the liquor, he let the tears flow down his face while Anita knocked around in the kitchen, pulling out coffee cups and sugar and cream, digging into her tin for left-over fruit cake.

When he felt like starting back up the hill, Corry pulled on his heavy coat, scarf, cap, and the gloves Anita had given him. He pulled open the door, and the wind blew in such a pile of snow and ice that it scratched his face and shoved him back against the wall. Anita, suddenly beside him, leant her buxom weight to his, and they pushed to the door.

"You can't go out in that," she said. "There's too much of a blow. You'd never make it."

Corry shook his head. "No," he said. "I don't think I would."

"You'll spend the night here," Anita said firmly. "I'll get Cam up and make her sleep with me. You can have that room."

"I hate to trouble you," Corry stuttered.

"It's no trouble. Besides, Corry Alcorn, you'd do the same for me."

Corry waited by the dying fire for the niece to be got out of the spare bedroom, and the bed to be fixed up for him. Then, after the women had gone to bed, feeling very much a tired man, he undressed himself by the fire and went to the little girl's room, crawling into a bed that was still warm from her body.

The next morning, after a good breakfast of biscuits, fried ham, and eggs, he started out, a thoughtful man, up the hill to home. And Anita and Cam, bundled up and hand in hand, began the three-mile walk for the bus. Some of the way they went to-gether—enough that the bus driver, as he came along the road, wondered what a man's big footprints were doing in the packed down snow beside those of Anita Longer and her twelve-year-old niece Cam.

John Bellin, driver of the number-one bus, told E. J. Lott and
Wilson Thrasher, drivers of the two other county buses, when
they were warming their hands and lungs in the furnace room.
Bellin, Lott, and Wilson Thrasher laughed long and hard about
Anita Longer, a silver-haired widow of fifty-five, her niece Cam,
and those footprints in the snow.

"Evil be to he who evil thinketh," said Guthrie Slone, poking
about his furnace. "I'll have none of that talk in here, fellows.
You can take your smoke someplace else."

So the drivers went to lounge in the kitchen with the cooks,
and laugh with them about those footprints in the snow.

Bethel Salyers, who heard it from her mother who was cooking
that day with Mary Kinney, started teasing Cam on the playground. First she only hinted that she knew a secret. Then she
swore she couldn't tell what it was, but she let on that it was
something that Cam already knew. And, when Cam could not
take not knowing any longer, Bethel turned on her, teasing and
taunting, and saying the nasty things that older girls say to
younger ones.

In tears, Cam ran to her aunt and cried out the lies they had
teased her with, telling all the things that she did not understand
but thought she should be offended by.

On Tuesday morning, when the break in the weather came,
Corry Alcorn set out to town for the supplies he needed. Walking
briskly, his big boots plodding through the gravel and soggy
muck of his meadows, he threw back his shoulders and thought
of what a fine winter day it was going to be. The cold, clinging
air slapped his face and made him alert to the brilliance of God's
world. He thought it had been a long time since he had last been
to church. As soon as the signs were favorable, and he could get
the truck out of the yard where it was sunk in and stuck, he
would go. He thought of Bill, lonely in the city, going to church
on Christmas. It no longer hurt to think of Bill and his wife. He
was glad for them now. It didn't take away his loneliness but still
he could be glad.

"I should write to Bill," he thought suddenly. "I should write
him today, and mail the letter while I'm in town."

So he decided to stop off at Yellowhawk and ask Anita Longer to make him up a short letter. Anita would remember Bill's address. She never forgot things like that.

When the tall man with cap in hand knocked on the door of the principal's office and asked to see Miss Longer, the women teachers lounging in the office store turned their heads and snickered. Then they gave in to their curiosity and went ahead and stared while Anita was being fetched.

When she saw him, and them watching her, Anita could not hold back the blush. It stole up her face and smothered her because she knew what they were thinking. Then, their snickering angered her and she flushed even harder. Corry Alcorn wondered if she was running a fever. He thought of bringing her some medicine from town.

"Hello, Corry," Anita said at last.

"Hello," Corry said. "I'm sorry to bother you, but I wondered..." and he explained about the letter.

"Sure," Anita said. "I'll write it for you." She went to her pocketbook hanging on the wall rack of the office. She took out a pen. Then she got a sheet of paper and an envelope from the store of school supplies, dropping in two cents to cover the charge for the stationery. She pulled out a chair for herself and one for Corry. She put her paper on a book and held it on her lap, writing quickly the words that Corry stumbled out, a little slowly, a little hesitantly, flushing himself because he was embarrassed for these people to know that he could not read or write.

When he was gone, Anita pulled herself up to her full widow's height. She threw back her shoulders and gave every woman in the office lounge a cold stare. And without a word, she went back to her room.

That afternoon, Bethel Salyers and her friends started teasing Cam again.

In their heaviest coats and boots, Anita and Cam made their way up the hill on Friday night to Settlor's Breach. The white frame house was slick and shiny from thawed water trickling down its sides all day. The moon lighting up the little buildings around made it seem strangely like a fort perched here, in this lone, unsettled stretch of land, a fort defending itself and the people within from something strange and unknown and unreal.

Corry was surprised to see them. He had never had many visitors, never any women. He cleared away his supper dishes, and stoked up the fire. He found two chairs for them, and pulled them up close to the hearth. Anita let Cam warm herself before she sent her into the kitchen to study, and told her to close the door behind her.

"I'm sorry to come in on you this way," Anita said slowly. "But I always figured you were a fine man and a good neighbor and I could trust you. Now I've got something awful to tell you, something wicked and untrue and filthy dirty. If it were just myself that it hurt, or even you, I wouldn't come telling it. But it's because of her," and Anita dropped her voice, "that I've come."

Corry pulled his own chair closer to Anita's and listened quietly, wondering what had made Anita Longer come out at night and come to him.

"You know who Cam is," she asked.

"Your niece," Corry said.

"No, she was Ed's daughter. Born out of wedlock to a wild woman who brought her to our porch when she was four days old and left her there. Ed didn't want her. He said she was to go to an orphanage. He didn't want the evidence of his shame around him. That's what he said."

She stopped for a moment, drew breath, and then went on. "I loved the little girl from the minute I laid eyes on her. I took her in, and I said to Ed, she'll stay. That's the only time in our marriage I ever talked back to him. I let it be known that Cam was the daughter of my sister who'd died in childbirth. I said I'd gone up to Michigan to fetch her. No one ever questioned me. I don't know if people knew Ed's ways or not. Anyway, if they did, they kept their mouths shut and didn't say a word. I've raised Cam. When Ed died, we kept on together. I'll keep her until she's old enough for college. I intend to send her there myself.

"She's a good girl and a proud girl. And I don't want her to ever know about who she was those four days before she came to me."

Corry nodded his head, saying nothing.

"But now," Anita sighed, "now there's a danger that she'll be told—that people are going to talk. I'm sure there's some who know the kind of man Ed was. Mind you, I'm not saying he wasn't a good man—he was kind and good to me. But he had his ways. There's people here who know that I never loved him, nor him me, but that we were married because our parents wanted it that way. I was only seventeen when I married him, and he was thirty-five. That's a lot of difference. His ways were set. And they didn't include much of me. But I was true to him through it all. And after he died, I've lived there alone with Cam."

Then she told him what they were saying at Yellowhawk, about her and about him, and about how Cam came home crying on the bus each day.

Corry Alcorn's face turned red. His ears pricked up, and his adam's apple bobbed angrily. His eyes flashed, his calm open hands folded into angry tough-looking fists. He looked at Anita Longer, and he looked toward his kitchen door where Cam was studying up for Monday's classes.

For a long time there was silence. Neither one spoke out his thoughts, thoughts that were ticking along fast in the passing minutes, and their breathing grew louder as each looked at the other, uncertain as to what could or should be said. At last Corry Alcorn broke the stillness, saying his piece as quietly as melted ice slides down a rain pipe, making puddles in the thawing snow.

"Anita," he said, "I'm a man of forty-six. I've little to offer but myself, my house, and my land. But I'd be proud if you'd share it all as my wife."

Anita could not look up, could not meet the blue eyes of the man who had just asked to marry her.

"I've only my girl," she said at last.

"And to have her as my daughter," Corry said, as if he were continuing a sentence.

Still she said nothing.

"It's not because I feel sorry for you," Corry said at last. "It's not because I feel like the whole matter was my fault, barging in on you the way I did that night. It's because I'm a lonely man, and I like you very much. I'd like to do what Bill did—find some- one who could be happy with me."

"I could be happy," Anita whispered. "Thank you, God," she muttered under her breath. "Thank you very much."

Corry reached out and touched her hand. From the kitchen they could hear sounds of Cam spelling out loud, going over and over each word, pronouncing it carefully, spelling it slowly to herself, then looking away and trying to spell from memory. Her voice grew louder as they sat, afraid to break their stillness, just listening to the uncertain voice of the girl who was eagerly grasping for the perfection of each word.

XV

It was a Friday night, so warm and misty that it made Carol's throat ache. She felt like a small rain-ruffled bird, crouched in her nest, wanting to join in the night chorus of summer winds drumming against black tree trunks to the rhythm of the moonlight. But she was afraid...afraid that the crickets and bullfrogs and ring-eyed owls would cock their heads and laugh when she missed a low note of their lonesome song.

So she sat rocking in the green swing, dragging herself across the porch with one foot; pushing, swinging backward, pushing, swinging backward.

"It's always this way for me," she thought. "I give myself a little push, and for a minute or two, I'm up in the high winds right under the moon. Then I fall back."

She stopped suddenly, bumping against the side of the clapboard house. "Ouch," she cried, and murmured under her breath, "that was just Life back there, giving me one of her jars."

"What's the matter, Carol?" called Grandpa from the living room. By the porch light, she could see his silhouette against the patched rosebud wallpaper—the long, proud bearded face, the last month's newspaper held far out from his squinted-up eyes, even the rim of his suspender straps.

"Nothing," she yelled back. She sighed, pulled a hollyhock from the trellis, and gave herself another push.

"Good evening, Carol."

She looked up. It was Ray Miller letting himself through the gate. Now what would he be wanting here in the hollow on a summer evening?

"Hello, Ray," she said, trying to sound neighborly. She didn't take much to Ray Miller any more. They had grown up together,

back when he and his family lived in the hollow. But then the
Millers moved across the river. "I've got to have a bigger pay-
check," Ray Miller's father had said. "I have a family to support."
He took a job in a shoe factory and his wife Sally started clerking
in one of the big department stores. Now Ray Miller stood uncertainly on the porch steps, smelling of the city, holding a box in
one hand.

"You want me to call Grandpa?" Carol asked.

"Don't trouble yourself," he said. "I was just visiting and
thought I'd stop by for a few minutes and see how you were getting along, Carol."

"Well enough."

"Glad to hear it. Mind if I sit down?"

"Go ahead."

He sat down beside her in the swing.

"Who is it, Carol?" Grandpa called out.

"Ray Miller, sir," Ray answered. Carol thought his voice
trembled a bit.

"Oh. Well, mind you don't ketch cold, Carol, from sitting in
the dark too long."

"No, Grandpa."

After a minute or two, Ray looked over at her. "That's a pretty
flower you've got there, Carol."

"This? It's just a hollyhock." She held it out and spun it around
in her long sunburned fingers. "How can you find it pretty, Ray?
The buds aren't even opened up, and it's all wet with dew."

Ray took the flower and pressed it between his hands. "How do
I find it pretty? Just because you picked it, for one reason. You
must have seen something lovely in it."

"I was just lonesome. A flower's better company than nothing."
Then she bit her lip. She shouldn't have said that. She wouldn't
have Ray thinking she lacked friends in the hollow, now that he
had moved away.

"Well," Ray sounded embarrassed, "I suppose so. I brought you
something," he added abruptly.

She unfolded the drugstore wrapping paper carefully and took
out a long narrow box of candy. After-dinner mints.

"They're peppermint. Remember how you used to like peppermint at Yellowhawk?"

"Yes, I remember," she said slowly. "I saved up all the pennies Grandpa gave me to buy candy. Sometimes I didn't have a nickel. You didn't either. So we put our money together and bought a peppermint patty."

They sat there together, rocking back and forth, sucking on after-dinner mints and watching the fireflies flutter and flicker across the tall meadow grasses.

"Sometimes," Carol said thoughtfully, "I wish I were one of those lightning bugs. Then I could sleep all day and fly around after it was dark, seeing nothing but the black of night...unless I went sliding up and down a moon-beam shadow."

"You'd like that, wouldn't you, Carol?" Ray said. "So would I."

Carol looked up at him.

"Oh, it's not all you think it is, living in the city. Buying your groceries in a supermarket, going to a red-brick church every Sunday, having dinner at the restaurants. It's lonely there, too. Lonelier in the city than it is in the hollow, Carol. You may not believe that—you think I've got fancy friends with new cars and pretty sisters for me to take to parties. Maybe I have. But they're all empty people. I don't mean anything special to them. I'm just one of the crowd."

Carol leaned back and studied him from the corner of her eyes. "Why do you come telling all this to me, Ray Miller?"

"I don't know, Carol. Maybe it's because you've always been a gentle girl. Maybe because I just—always liked you."

She couldn't think of anything to say.

"Well," he sighed. "I've been so busy talking about myself I haven't really asked about you. How have you been, now that your mother died?"

"That was two years ago, Ray," she said quietly. "Don't come asking me about Mom now. You didn't bother to come up then, when I could have used a kind word. So don't offer me one now." She turned her head aside. "Since then, Joy's died of fever. The welfare lady came and took Tom and Clarence. She said this wasn't a fit place for them to live, with just Grandpa and me to care for them, and him at work all day...and carrying on strange-like half the night.

"She'd have taken me, too, but Grandpa lied about my age. So did the neighbors. It'd have broken Grandpa's heart if we all left him. It would have broken mine, too. I don't think I could stand living away from the hollow."

Ray put his hand on her arm and then looked away. "Carol," he said, "I'm sorry to hear it all. I didn't know...I didn't have any idea things had got that bad."

"Don't be sorry, Ray," she said. "I don't think it matters any more. I'm beat down now. It's got me."

In the quiet they could hear Carol's grandpa wheezing as he raised himself from his chair and took down the banjo. He held it up against his thick rough body and began to strum slowly, half crooning, half sobbing to himself.

Carol shivered as she listened. It always frightened her when her grandpa acted this way. He only knew one song, which he played over and over, singing the words as he made them up. Carol said the song was made up of echoes of her youth. It reminded her of the only happy days she had ever known, when they had all been together in the little house.

Ray listened, too, with his head kind of hung over on one side, his eyes far beyond the moon.

"It saddens me, Carol, to see you and your Grandpa this way," he said, when the song was finished. "I think it's these hills. They've done something to you. It's as if they took away your dreams and left you living in a world so real it's almost make-believe. I wish you'd leave them, Carol. I wish you'd leave the hollow and come to the city with me."

"Why, Ray Miller," Carol said, drawing out each word on a separate breath. "Whatever are you saying?"

"Please come with me. I know you don't think you'd ever be happy away from here. And I've said how lonely the city was. But it would be different if we were together. We could find our way. I'm sure of it."

"The way we found a way to buy that candy, Ray?"

"Yes. We could scrape together the bits and pieces of our lives, the way we used to gather up pennies. Maybe we could make one solid nickel out of the whole mess." He laughed self-consciously at his little joke.

Carol smiled. "You've a pretty way of putting things, Ray," she said. "And you've got a good idea, maybe. One I'll toy with. But I can make you no promises. Why, what would I do without this hollow? What would become of Grandpa?"

"It's time to think of yourself, Carol," Ray said carefully. "You're sixteen, now, and what do you do? Each day you work in those fields until your hands are raw and your back aches. You've got no friends here, and you'll likely make none. You've lost your sister, and brothers, not to mention a mother who died of hard work. You've never been beyond the eighth grade of Yellowhawk."

"Could I get more schooling in your town, Ray?"

"I'd teach you myself," he said with a smile. "That's what I do now, you know. I'm a teacher at the high school." He reached for her hand. "Please, Carol."

"Oh, no, Ray," she said. "I couldn't go. Besides, I've got no place there to stay."

"Carol," he pleaded. "I'm asking you to marry me, to be my wife." He reached to the porch floor and picked up the fallen flower. "Here you are now," he said, holding up the tight little bud. "A beautiful flower—with all your blossoms closed and pressed against you. You've been torn from the vine; you've been drifting in the wind. Now it's time for you to settle. Do you fall into a pile of dried-up wilted leaves, or do you spring up again from fresh soil, to spread your petals to the wind?"

"He's right, Carol," said a tired voice from the doorway. "I've been listening." Grandpa walked to the porch steps and stood breathing of the heavy night air, his face turned up toward the hills and the hill cemetery he knew well. "Your mom would want it this way. She'd say, 'Dad, tell the girl to go. It's time for her to leave, and Ray Miller is as good as any boy who'll take her.' She'd smile up at me with those blue eyes of hers and say 'Go tell her, Dad.' And I'd come, just like I came now. Who knows?" He shook his head. "Maybe she is whispering in my ear right now. Maybe that's why..." his shoulders slumped and he leaned against the railing.

Carol stood up slowly. "I'll get my things, Ray. I'll come with you tonight, or not at all."

Ray smiled. "I'll be waiting on the ridge. You'll want to say good-by to your grandpa."

"Take care of her," the big man called to the shadow on the path.

"Grandpa?"

"Yes?"

"Take these." She handed him the flower and the box of candy.

"I don't need these to remember you by, if that's what you're thinking," he said. "I'll not forget my own dead daughter's girl. You keep them. You keep them to help you remember all you left behind tonight."

"I'll not forget either," Carol thought, walking backward against the wind, listening to her grandpa's song. But from the shadow on the porch to the shadow on the ridge, she could hear only one line, half sung, half whispered, over and over again, echoes of her youth.

❧XVI❧

Arnaldis stretched and yawned and tried to enjoy her lazy feeling. After all, she hadn't done nothing, nothing at all but wade the rapids looking for tadpoles and splashing the water up and down under her bare feet. ("Always wear your old tennis shoes in the creek, honey," Annie would say over and over, time and again. "Otherwise you'll get your feet cut up on sharp rocks. Or broken bottles." But who could wear shoes to wade the rapids on a warm spring day?) Then she had stretched out on a flat yellow rock under the bridge, looking up at sparrows that seemed to shoot through the clouds into a clear blue sky. She just needed time to be by herself and think. She wanted time to lie out like old Huck Finn and digest what the world's about, and what it's coming to. Time to think about Mom dying after she'd run off with another man. Time to try to forget it. Time to tell herself that she, Arnaldis Young, didn't have to turn out that way; time enough for her to convince herself that she could feel things like that, and say them, without being disrespectful to her mom's memory.

In the late afternoon, a fat girl in short shorts came out of the camp across the creek and began to toast marshmallows. Arnaldis watched her pull them off the stick and pop them into her fat mouth. What was that girl thinking about? Could she look over and see Arnaldis laying there watching her and pretending that she was with old Huck Finn, ready for adventure on the Mississippi? Arnaldis watched until the sweet smoky smell made her hungry and sick at the same time. Then she finished her cherry pop, warm and cheap from Bartlett's store, but cold from the creek waters where she had kept it, closed her eyes, and let herself melt into an underwater world of ice crystals, soggy frozen cattails, and Huck Finn on a raft that hugged the river bottom and kept him from being seen above by the spies staked out along the shores of the Mississippi.

Now Arnaldis knew that she was a dreamer and a disappointment to her dad, who wanted her to grow up and go to college to become a teacher before she came back here to settle down for life and marry the boy next door. (She guessed that's who it'd be. Right now there wasn't a boy next door, only the Kidwells with five girls). Arnaldis knew that she was a dreamer and she'd probably never amount to anything because she was already fifteen years old and wouldn't study or do anything right. But she just liked to get away by herself to think it all over, even the things she'd already thought over a hundred times or so. She couldn't help it, could she, if she was a born dreamer and that's the way she was?

Then when she saw night coming, little white stars told her it was here as they slipped through the blue sky, past the sparrows, and strained their eyes down to earth, she knew it was time for her to tell Huck to shove off so she could pack up and start home. Huck and she hadn't got too far on the river that day, and they hadn't done much talking, but Arnaldis had done a lot of thinking and she felt good about it all. But she was still worried at the thoughts of going home. You see, how could she tell Annie that she'd wasted another Saturday? How could she tell Annie that she'd left her books at the foot of the bridge and headed down to the creek where she could just lie back and let her head be free of all this talk, all this big talk that Annie and Daddy did when they sat back and planned her life.

Annie was fine, though, and Arnaldis guessed she really ought to call her Aunt Annie since she was Mom's sister and had lived with them ever since Mom died. Annie was fine, but she didn't understand. She was a worker, and a mover—hands busy, mouth always full of words, head dizzy with ideas that she'd got to make come true. Like Arnaldis' becoming a teacher. Annie just didn't understand how that girl could spend a Saturday afternoon sitting by the creek and daydreaming if she was going to become a schoolteacher (after graduating from college Phi Beta Kappa) and making her and Delmar proud.

Arnaldis couldn't hold this against her, though. Annie just wanted to do right by her sister's daughter because Silvie would have been so proud to have a smart daughter, a grown-up smart daughter schoolteacher. "It's a good job," Annie kept telling Arnaldis. "It pays good, you get time off, and it's respectable. Even more than that, it's giving something of yourself back to the land that begot you."

But Arnaldis didn't know. She hadn't taken the time to think it all through because it bothered her. It was something she didn't really want to think about, because she couldn't think much beyond her mom's dying and the preacher saying Ashes to Ashes and Dust to Dust—wasn't this giving something of yourself back to the land that begot you? But wasn't it giving too much?

This kind of thinking bothered Annie and Daddy; Arnaldis knew it did because they didn't really want her to think about what they told her was Right and Good. It bothered them, too, because Arnaldis could let herself not think about it, because she could sit back and dream for a whole day and not once let her future cross her mind.

So, when she got home, she didn't tell Annie where she'd been or what she'd done. She made up a story, she told a lie even though she knew she shouldn't do that. She knew she should of gone right ahead and told them the truth, but somehow she couldn't. It was better to hear them jar at her for something they thought she'd done but she hadn't than have them digging at her thoughts and trying to find out what was on her mind.

So she made up a fantastic lie, a dreamer's story about a boy called Bo Howard driving her thirty miles to the state park where blue boats skim up and down in the cold water, racing each other against their shadows. She told Annie and Daddy about an old man scooping water out of his rowboat with a rusty bean can and little kids running around in polkadot sunsuits, soaking up sun on their scrawny bellies. She told them about a little girl who jumped in the water and her dad had to go get her out while the mother just stood on the grass and screamed Hurry Joe Hurry, she's drowning.

"State park, huh?" said Delmar, looking Arnaldis over and shaking his head. "State park, you say now?"

"Yes, sir."

"My, my. Any drinking going on out there?"

"No, sir."

"I hear the place is one big dump for beer cans. I hear there're men whose never seen a woman in a bathing suit, just drive up and drink beer and gawk. You see any of those men?"

"No, sir."

"No man out there said anything out of line to you?"

"No, sir."

"Huh, now," he grunted, biting hard on his lip. He squinted from behind his glasses. "You look awful tired."

"What do you mean, Daddy?"

"I mean you look awful tired to have had that kind of an easy day."

"Shame on you, Delmar," Annie said. "You stop that kind of talk. I know what you mean, you evil-thinking man, but that child doesn't know what you're saying."

"I don't believe that," Delmar said, looking at his daughter but seeing Silvie Young and Hogarth Evans standing there before him, laughing and crying at the same time. "I don't believe that."

Arnaldis stared hard at them both, choking back the hurt. There he had done it again. Maybe Delmar couldn't help it, but he always hurt her. Any time he couldn't understand something or thought—knew—she wasn't telling him the truth, he would start at her this way. I shouldn't of made up the story, she thought, and I shouldn't of said I was with a boy. It was mean of me, I guess, as well as being a sin.

But how could she trust Delmar with the truth? He didn't trust her just because Mom ran away with Hogarth Evans and lived with him three months before she died. Delmar didn't think she knew about Mom and Hogarth, but she did. She had heard it from the kids at school and it had broken her heart. She came home crying and Annie said, "What's wrong?" and she had told her and asked if it was true. Annie had said yes, Delmar was carrying on so because his Silvie was dying that Silvie just couldn't stand it any more. Delmar kept her up nights crying and asking her what he was to do once she was gone, and Silvie would say Delmar, I just don't know, can't you leave me in peace for the time I've got left? Then Delmar would cry more until Silvie couldn't stand it any more. So one night she put Arnaldis in bed and kissed her and then called Hogarth who had been in love with her since they went to grade school together and Hogarth said yes, he'd come. So while Delmar was at the Masonic Lodge, Hogarth Evans came for Silvie and they went off in his pick-up truck to the fishing camp Hogarth kept somewhere in Ohio. Silvie stayed there with him until she died, and then Hogarth called Annie like Silvie had asked him to, and Annie took Delmar's car and went for her. Delmar wouldn't go, he wouldn't face Hogarth, he stayed at home and cried and told Arnaldis that her mom had died in the sanitarium up in Ohio. When Annie told Arnaldis about it, she told her everything because she said it was better that Arnaldis knew the truth from her than heard what stories the kids at school might make up.

Arnaldis had asked her what had become of Hogarth, that sometime she might want to go and talk to him, but Annie said that was awful, what he had done was sinful even if he had loved her mom and tried to make her happy before she died. Annie said he'd have to answer to God when the time came and her sister Silvie, Arnaldis' mom, was already answering so Arnaldis should just try to be a good girl and study hard and grow up to be a schoolteacher so that Delmar would have some pride again and people here wouldn't say Like Mother, Like Daughter.

But it hurt Arnaldis when her daddy looked at her that way, like he'd first started looking at her when she was ten years old and he'd told her that Silvie had gone into the sanitarium. And now she wished that she'd not made up the story about Bo Howard, what a ridiculous name, and the trip to the state park. She wished she had just told them both that she'd hid her books and sat out in the creek banks, wasting the day enjoying spring, not thinking much at all, just dreaming about going down the Mississippi River on a raft with Huck Finn and never coming back to Yellowhawk.

Arnaldis knew that what she'd done was awful, and she was getting sorrier and sorrier. She knew that she would have to answer to God for all her lies and it almost scared her to death, because she wondered what had happened to Mom after she died; had God sent her to hell because she'd lived three months in a fishing camp with Hogarth?

So she went to her room and sat on the edge of her bed shaking. She told herself over and over again that if she ever had another chance she wouldn't tell Daddy and Annie another lie. She said a little prayer to God and told him the same thing. Then she asked him to please be good to her mom, Silvie Young, because she'd only done what must have seemed best to her at the time, and like the preacher said when he spoke out at her funeral, we're only human and to err is human but to forgive, divine, so please, God, forgive Silvie Young. "And forgive me, too," Arnaldis said, "and I will try once more to be your humble servant and do only what is Good and Right even if it is what Annie and Daddy tell me to do." Then she tried to make a bargain with God, even though the preacher said that we should not try to strike up compacts with the Lord because we must give him everything. Arnaldis told the Lord that if he would forgive Mom and Hogarth Evans and her—all three—she would try to study hard and even be a schoolteacher and live here in Yellowhawk instead of dreaming of adventure. Then she bit her lip and said, "I don't know for sure if I can stop dreaming altogether, Lord, but I'll try." And that was her bargain.

Arnaldis bowed her head and sat very still after she had said Amen, biting her lip the way Delmar bit his when he wasn't sure about something. She asked God if maybe he could find time to send her a sign, and she said she'd sit where she was and wait for a while in case he found the time to do just that. She kept her eyes closed, and sat very still and waited.

Finally she opened her eyes and looked around, but she was still in the same room at the top of the stairs, the room across the hall from Annie's and down the way from Delmar's. The room was just the same, same paper, same furniture, same picture of Mom in a dime-store frame on the dresser. As she looked at the picture of Mom, and tried not to cry, she saw the package sitting beside it.

Oh, she thought, that's it. Thank you, God, thank you for helping me remember. Thank you for sending me a sign.

She jumped off the bed and kissed the package, she was so

happy that God had heard. Then she went running down the stairs, back into the kitchen where Delmar and Annie were still sitting at the table, each of them looking down into the empty spots where their plates had been.

"Happy Birthday, Annie," Arnaldis said. "Happy Birthday! I'm sorry if it's the end of the day, and it seems late, but Happy Birthday."

"Why, Arnaldis," Annie purred, her hands shaking as she reached across the empty coffee pot to take the box. "How sweet of you, how sweet. You're the only one who remembers my birthday now that your mom is gone and I don't have a mother of my own any more. You're the only one."

Annie snapped off the blue ribbon and tore into the rosebud paper. "Lavendar soap," she said. "Oh, doesn't it smell good? Smell it, Delmar."

"Yes." Delmar's lip quivered.

He's remembering Mom, Arnaldis thought. He's remembering how she used to get this at Rexall when she had enough money. He's remembering how he hated for her to spend the money for what he said was sinful and unfit to put before the Lord. I shouldn't have got the soap, she thought. I should have got something else. I never do anything right.

"Arnaldis, you must have got this at the drugstore," Delmar said.

"Yes, I did."

"Oh, I thought so," Annie purred. "It's real good soap—toilet soap like your mom used to use. I always wanted some, but I never felt that I could splurge on it." She shot a look at Delmar. "I never felt it was right to spend Delmar's money to such things when you were in want or this house was in need of fixing up."

Delmar looked up at Annie with a hurt look in the pale eyes that shone out behind his glasses. "Now, Annie," he said, "I've never grudged you a penny. I've never asked you once how you spent my money. Isn't that right?"

"Well, Delmar ..."

"There's nothing you've ever asked for, within reason, that you didn't get, you or Arnaldis. Or Silvie, God rest her soul. Deny that, deny it if you can."

"I'm not reproaching you, Delmar. I'm just saying I never felt it was right to spend your hard-earned money on such luxuries as these when Arnaldis would soon be needing all the money we've got to send her to college."

Delmar was quiet for a minute. Then, "Arnaldis won't go to college," he said, with a sigh. "Just look at her. She's not the type. She's too much like your sister. Like mother, like daughter. She's going to grow up making trips to the state park with Bo Howard or his likes, and she'll spend every cent she can find on stuff that isn't fit to be put before the Lord on a Sunday morning. And do you know what will happen to her?"

"Don't, Delmar, don't..." Annie's face was drawn up like an overcooked apple and her mouth was screwed in at the corners. She had started this fight, but she was getting mad over the way it was going. And she looked a lot like Delmar when she got mad, except that she didn't wear glasses.

"I'll tell you what will happen to her..."

Hearing them starting to jar at each other had worn Arnaldis out. She wanted to slip away, back upstairs to sit on the edge of her bed and tell God that if that had been the sign he'd sent her, it hadn't been a very good one. Or else she had misused it.

"Where do you think you're going?"

"Up to my room."

"What for? Not to study?"

"No, not to study. Oh, I don't know," Arnaldis cried. "Have I got to account for every movement I make?" Like my mother, she wanted to say.

"In this house, you do. As long as you're living under my roof, I've a right to know everything you do. And think," Delmar roared.

"No," Arnaldis said, and she was sobbing now. "No, Daddy, you don't. I'm a good girl and I try to do what you and Annie tell me. I try to let you run my life and say nothing about it. But I won't tell you everything I do, and I won't tell you what I think. You wouldn't want me to. You wouldn't want me to tell you that I wonder night and day why my mother left you, why you couldn't make her happy enough that she wanted to stay here with you and die in your arms, with me at her side. You..."

Delmar half rose out of his chair, slow like, lifting up his left hand. "You evil spawn of the devil," he said. "How can you say such things to your father? Your soul is in danger of hell damnation and you stand there and dare to sass me, your father, who gave you life and kept that life going when even your own mother didn't think enough of you to stay by your side."

"Oh, Delmar," Annie cried, "Delmar, that's too much."

"No, Daddy," Arnaldis wailed, and at the same time she said I'm sorry, God, I didn't mean it to come out this way. "No, it wasn't you who raised me, it was her. She's the one who has taken care of me, and you, too, and tried to show us that we're still people, we have a right to be proud and free."

Arnaldis was crying then, and Annie was crying, too, as she came across the room and put her arms around the girl. "You beautiful child," she said, and Arnaldis cried harder because no one had called her beautiful after Mom had left. "You beautiful child, I didn't know you loved me."

Delmar was trembling, he was so mad. Once Arnaldis thought he was going to hit them both, but Annie stepped between and hid the girl behind her big body.

"She's Silvie's girl, Delmar," Annie said. "Like mother, like daughter. And you should be proud. You ought to shout and pray and give thanks when you see her so happy and healthy, so full of life, so forgiving."

Delmar turned away and Arnaldis bowed her head.

"Let her be, Delmar, let her have her fun. It won't last long enough—it never does, once a girl gets to this age. Let her go. Let her have her fun, let her go with Bo Howard. Let her be."

Arnaldis was hugging Annie, clinging to her and asking God to help her, help her tell them there wasn't any Bo Howard, she was just a dreamer sitting on the creek bank thinking of Huck Finn and wondering if she would ever see the Mississippi.

"Let her be, Delmar," Annie said again.

"Vipers, a den of vipers, and I live in their midst," Delmar moaned. "I'm only thankful her mother didn't live to see this day. She may have destroyed her own body, but this would have destroyed her soul. But then, what would your kind know of souls?"

"I know about souls," Arnaldis hummed, slipping quietly out the kitchen door, leaving them standing there together. "There are many kinds. There is the soul of the butterfly glowing moonlight on a snowy night, in the dead of winter, when all but God thinks that the butterfly is dead. There is the soul of spring, stuck in each breath drawn from a pine tree. There is the soul of my mother, white, cold, gleaming with its own goodness...the soul fashioned by the hand of God, giving itself back to God in the only way it knew how, in love."

On she went, wandering slowly down the path of Bright April Valley. On she went, in the dark, thinking to herself tomorrow is another day. Another day to fill with thoughts and smells and feelings. Tomorrow she'd go back to the rapids and wade in the spring cold water. Maybe one of those sparrows would fly down and sing to her. Maybe that same fat girl would come out of her camp and roast marshmallows again. If she did, this time Arnaldis would leave Huck Finn and go to talk to her. If the fat girl talked back, maybe her voice would be kind and gentle and full of friendly laughter.

And when she went home in the evening, she wouldn't make up a story for Delmar and Annie. She'd tell them where she'd been and what she'd done. She'd even tell them what her thoughts had been, if they wanted to know. And then maybe Delmar would laugh, maybe he would see how silly and harmless his daughter was, just a dreamer. Maybe he would sit back and laugh and not bite out at them any more.

But today. Today had been Annie's birthday, and Arnaldis was the only one who remembered. Not even Delmar had bought her a present, and she'd lived with them for five years and taken care of them. It was bound to be a lonely day, a lonely birthday, the same every year from now until she died. No wonder Annie would often say, "Safe in the arms of Jesus, sweet Lord," and sigh. Only there would she find peace and love and the happiness that she had thought she could find on earth.

Arnaldis walked on for a while, then she went back to the house. She helped Annie clear away the dishes and straighten up the kitchen. The quarrel was forgotten, Delmar sat in his straight chair looking through the newspapers that lay on his lap. The quarrel was forgotten, all the things that they said over and over to each other every night.

Arnaldis kissed them both good night, and picked up her books from the table. She went up to her room and closed the door and started to study. She made her dreams go away, she said another prayer to God and asked him to help her think straight and not daydream over her books any more. She had to study, she had to learn. She had to make something of herself, so she could go away to college and see what the world was like outside of Yellowhawk. Then maybe she would even want to come back, be a schoolteacher, and marry the boy next door if there was one by then. Then maybe people would look at her and smile and remember Silvie Young when she was young and pretty and smart and taught school here, long ago before she married Delmar and had Arnaldis and found out she was dying and ran away with Hogarth Evans. Maybe then they would look at Arnaldis, so good and pretty, and remember her mom as she'd been then—and smile and say Like Mother, Like Daughter.

XVII

Fred Marble was the one who came back from East Keyhoe telling what he had seen at Skinny Fork. At first, nobody believed
him and they all told him to go hush. Jewell Tackitt said no one
ought to be allowed to go around spreading tales like that, it was
a nuisance to decent people who stayed at home and minded their
own business. But Jewell Tackitt's ears were burning and she
cocked her head in Fred's direction every time he came in sight,
hovering like a cockroach to pick up any scandalous crumbs of
gossip.

Otis Seagraves said it was all a lot of nonsense, too, and Fred
ought to have his eyes examined or his tongue tightened up. Fred
bit his lip and told Otis to go and see for himself. So Otis went.

One fine Sunday morning, he hitchhiked down 42, getting a
ride with a farmer on his way to the stockyards. The farmer let
Otis off at East Keyhoe, and set Otis to walking past Johnson's
15-cent hamburger cafe, over the half-paved, half-graveled road
to Skinny Fork.

With shiny black eyes that glittered and crackled in the sunny
wind, Otis took in all the newness of the lower end of the county.
And he began to wonder if maybe there wasn't some truth to
what Fred Marble had told. He didn't like the feel of things here.
He didn't like the way people lived, crowded up together like
they were afraid to be alone with their own little pieces of grass
and stars, smelling their own brand of smoked wind, seeing the
moon rise on a path above its own notched-out hill. Otis didn't
like the sloth, either. He wondered what Jack Riggs and his wife
Helen would say if they saw the way people lived down here. He
wondered if maybe he shouldn't tell them, just to let them know

how lucky they were to have settled on Dummit Road instead of moving. He knew now why Helen's mother had forbidden her daughter to move the ten miles away. She had said it would be sending her daughter to perdition, to have her move down county. People had laughed at her; said she was set in her ways. Helen had cried and begged. Jack Riggs had pleaded with his mother-in-law. But she said no. And they built their house on Dummit Road, right down the bend from the old lady. The neighbors had felt sorry for Helen, and tried to make her feel at home there. But they felt a little funny toward her, too, for trying to move away from them. Otis thought that sometime he would stop by and tell Helen how right her mother had been.

Otis shook his head and clicked his teeth, making a little noise like a cricket warming up to chew on a pair of nylons. He passed another yard full of children. They stared at him with their wide, solemn eyes and did not smile back when he waved. Otis thought he liked the bawling, fighting, tag-playing ruckus his nieces and nephews made when they got a chance to play, more than the stillness of these piney-faced, spindly-armed youngsters.

Skinny Ridge road narrowed and forked. Otis wondered which way he should go. The sun was high now, and he was hot. Sweat was puckering at the neck of his blue shirt, and deepening the color under his arms.

He stood, staring hard at the road, when from behind he heard the roar of an approaching car. He stepped to one side, and held up his arm, ready to flag down the driver and ask the way. But the blue Ford, filled to the brim with laughing men and women, sped by him and covered him with hot, flaky swirls of dust. Otis clenched his jaw and wiped himself off as well as he could. The sound of another car coming fast sent him into the greenness of the meadow. He waved, but again no one stopped.

Two more cars came, following the road the first had taken. Reluctantly, Otis set out behind them, dancing along in the graveled ruts, skipping over to the side when still another automobile came barreling down the dirt road, its load of passengers laughing and looking out the windows.

Otis thought, I wonder if this is the way Fred Marble walked that day. He was beginning to wish he'd asked Fred to come along.

Then, in the distance, once he had rounded Dead Man's Curve and climbed down the slope that separated him completely from the East Fork territory, he saw the line of blue and green and black cars chugging along slowly, one behind the other, creeping down the dirt road. His curiosity began to itch him. Otis sped up his lope to a long-paced walk, just breaking on a run. He was soon to the end of the line. Only two people were in this car, a man and his wife.

"Howdy," Otis said, sticking his head in the back rolled-down window.

The man turned and stared back at Otis. His wife, her head ducked, darted a swift glance out of the corner of her eye.

"Turn around, Belle," her husband said. "No telling who it is. It might even be one of them."

Blushing a deep rose, the woman hastily turned to the window and began breathing in deep-throated gulps of hot dusty air.

"What do you want?" the man said at last.

Surprised by his coldness, Otis pulled his head out and stuck his hands into his pockets. "I was just wondering," he said, "if you could tell me if this is the way to..."

"It is," said the man sharply, and pushing his foot on the accelerator, he drove on.

Up ahead, there was a sudden loud burst of shrill laughter. "I see one," someone shouted. "I see one!"

"Where?" A man jumped out of the car behind and ran ahead a few feet.

"Over there," the man in the first car hollered. "Over there— see!"

"I see, I see." The man stumbled back to his car and began pointing to the people crowded in the back seat.

There was more laughter, louder and shriller.

The cars toward the rear began to be impatient. The man Otis had talked to gunned his motor and made a smoke stream and strong smell of gas. "Let's go," he shouted.

"Wait your turn, Brother Simmons," the woman driving a pick-up in front of him shouted back. "It won't be long."

Otis watched Brother Simmons turn fiery red and say something to his wife. He laid down strong on his horn.

There was a shout of protest from the motorists in front. "Let up," they cried. "You'll scare them all away."

But Brother Simmons only honked in faster, louder beep-beeps. The line began to creep along. Otis walked up beside the cars, listening to the laughter of the men and women craning their heads from the windows.

"You want to ride?" one person called. Otis turned and looked back, eagerly. But when he saw the people packed into the two-door sedan, he backed off.

"There's only eleven of us," one told him. "There's room for one more."

"You could sit on my lap," a woman shouted.

Her friends laughed.

Otis walked on, hastily, wondering what had got into them. Then, ahead, he saw. There on a slope of fresh grass, around a muddy little pond where cows were drinking and swishing their tails and chewing on their cuds, sat three men and one woman as naked as the day they were born. Otis, flushing bright red, looked away. Then he jerked his head back, his jaw working, his eyes blinking so he would not be blinded by the brightness of their flesh in the Sunday sun.

"You see 'em?" somebody called.

Otis nodded.

"Awful, isn't it?"

Otis looked. It was Brother Simmons and his wife, staring hard out their windows, her leaned across him and the steering wheel, panting hard.

"Well, I never," Mrs. Simmons said.

"Don't look, Belle," her husband told her.

"Oh, I won't." But Mrs. Simmons fixed her beady little stare on the four seated on the grass by the pond.

"What're they doing?" Otis asked.

"Reading scripture, so they say."

"Scripture?" Otis asked. "But I never..."

"Neither did I," Brother Simmons snapped.

"I should hope not," his wife gasped.

"This has got to be stopped," her husband said shortly. "Look at them all, how they enjoy it..." and he gestured to the cars in front of them. "They drive out here at least once a day, after work. They spend most all day Sunday parked on this road, watching. It's getting in their blood."

Just then, a little child led by its mother came out of the bushes and joined the four at the pond. One man stood up and helped them to sit down. There were loud catcalls and much honking from the cars parked in the road.

"Disgusting," Brother Simmons murmured.

Otis worked his jaw harder.

Then the little congregation sitting in the grass began to sing. They sang, loud and strong, a hymn about being washed in the blood of the lamb. No one in the cars joined them, but they didn't shout while there was any singing going on. A few more people came out of the bushes and sat down with them. One was an old man; there was a young woman, and her husband, and several children. Each time the singing stopped, the catcalls grew louder. So the group went from one hymn to the other, as fast as they could go.

Finally, their voices began to wear thin. Two of the men stood up, and waved them silent.

"That's the owners," Brother Simmons commented to Otis. "There's two of them—brothers. They started this place up about three weeks ago. It's been growing like sixty ever since."

The brothers offered up a prayer, and then one sat down.

The other, a big man covered with a coat of curly red hair that stretched down his back, and heavy, tanned legs, stayed standing, holding up a Bible in one hand.

"Talk a little louder," somebody shouted.

The preacher went on. Then he closed his Bible and took up a bottle from the grass. He took a drink from the bottle and passed it to the woman at his right. "'Rejoice and be glad, O daughter of Edom, that dwellest in the land of Uz; the cup also shall pass through unto thee; thou shalt be drunken, and shalt make thyself naked.'"

The bottle went around the circle, each man, woman, and child taking a sip.

From the road, there was quiet. Then more laughter. Then one man jumped out of his car and crossed the little ditch into the pasture. "I gotta see this," he was shouting. "It's too good to be true."

The people in his car shouted to him to come back, but he sprinted on across the meadow.

The preacher, ignoring the commotion behind him, cried out in a loud voice, " 'Neither is there any creature that is not manifest in his sight: but all things are naked and opened unto the eyes of him with whom we have to do.' " Then he whirled and faced the intruder, much to the dismay and amusement of the men and women watching from the road.

"Welcome, brother," he cried. "I am glad that you have seen the need to come to us. But I must ask you to remove your clothes, and appear naked in the eyes of the Lord and other believers."

The man laughed, and said something under his breath.

"Then you must leave, you are not among the chosen," the preacher said firmly.

Again, the man said something and took a step forward closer to the women in the group.

Two men, the preacher's brother and another, were at his side at once. "We must ask you to go," they said quietly.

"Or remove your clothing," the preacher added.

Hesitantly, the man lifted his foot and took another step into the group. At once, there were six strong arms reaching about him, grasping him in a grip of strong, muscly sinew.

"Take him out!" said the preacher.

They escorted him toward the road, the preacher following behind and crying in a loud voice, " 'So shall the king of Assyria lead away the Egyptian prisoners, and the Ethiopians captives, young and old, naked and barefoot, even with their buttocks uncovered, to the shame of Egypt.' "

Seeing the big, naked men coming closer, there were cries of protest from the women in the road.

The cars began to creep along, and after the man who had

caused the disturbance was put back into his seat, the line of traffic moved quickly.

The three nudists hurried back to their congregation.

"Why don't you build a fence?" someone cried as a parting jab.

"This is our land," the preacher's brother shouted back. "This is our place to gather. We are offending no one. Either go or join us."

"I'm going," cried the heckler, and he drove on.

Otis began to feel a little strange, with all the cars gunning their motors past him, covering him with the dust their spinning wheels dug out of the rutted road. He stood there, wiping himself of the thick, sticky shellac and batting his eyes to clear them. His ears were spinning from the closeness of the preacher's voice, crying, " 'Naked came I out of my mother's womb, and naked shall I return thither.' "

"Hear, hear," cried another. " 'As he came forth from his mother's womb, naked shall he return to go as he came, and shall take nothing of his labor, which he may carry away in his hand.' "

They were standing around him, when the dust cleared away. And one of them was whispering, " 'And there followed him a certain young man, having a linen cloth cast about his naked body; and the young men laid hold on him...and he left the linen cloth, and fled from them naked...' "

Thinking they were about to reach out for him, Otis turned and scurried off down the road as fast as he could, jumping the ditch and running in the soft green meadow cow paths.

When he was sure they were not behind him, chasing him, Otis stopped and collapsed on the grass, breathing hard and heavily, the sweat trickling down his face, mixing with tears of fright that he had squeezed out from the scare they gave him. He lay for a few minutes, face down. When he had caught his breath and raised himself up, he could hear somebody crying hard behind a tree.

"Who's there?" he cried. "Who's there?"

"Please help me," and a young girl stuck her head around the thick oak trunk. "I can't find my clothes, and I want to get out of here."

Otis jumped up and backed away a few steps.

"I won't hurt you," the girl sobbed. "I just want my clothes. I can't find them."

"Well, where did you take them off?" Otis asked. It was the only thing he could think of.

"Right in here," she said. "Come and help me look."

"Not on your life," Otis cried, and he started to run again.

"Oh, please help me," the girl stepped out and after him. "Or I'll never get home and my parents will wonder what's happened to me."

Otis felt the sweat breaking out afresh on the back of his neck. His hands began to tremble. His legs, he thought, were going to buckle under him. But they didn't. And he kept running, faster and faster, each heavy striding step taking him away from the crazy people on Skinny Fork.

Fred Marble was the one who brought the news about Lorraine Simmons, the fifteen-year-old girl from up Moon Creek, being caught by the sheriff when he came cruising past Skinny Fork late Sunday afternoon, checking the road for parkers.

"There she was," Fred said, "with not a stitch of clothing on her. Just sitting in the grass a-crying."

Jewell Tackitt said he shouldn't talk so. Amanda Colegrove told him to keep his mouth shut and to have more respect for the girl's family.

"Sheriff cleared out the whole bunch," Fred Marble said. "He took them all to jail. I wonder if he gave them time to get their clothes on."

Jewell Tackitt turned her head to smother a laugh.

"He fined the preacher and his brother $1,000," Fred told. "I wonder where they'll get the money to pay that."

"Maybe from the collection plate," Amanda snickered.

"I doubt that," Jewell whispered. "Where was they to keep their money, without any pockets on them?"

And they all laughed.

Fred went on about how awful it was for somebody from the upper end of the county to have got caught up in such a scandal. "Who would ever have thought it," he sighed, "about little Lorraine Simmons? As fine a girl as was ever raised here!"

"They shouldn't have sent her off to high school," Fred said. "Yellowhawk was enough. It was sending her on the bus to the lower end of the county. She's got strange ideas put in her head there."

Amanda and Jewell snickered. Fred turned to Otis Seagraves for support. "What do you think, Otis?" he asked.

But Otis would say nothing. He never did say much any more. He just walked around with his head cocked to one side and a funny dazed look on his face. People said he wasn't "right."

Otis said nothing, and kept his thoughts to himself. He didn't think it was a shame about Lorraine Simmons. He thought she had got what was coming to her. But Otis was careful where he walked at night. He was afraid of someone jumping out of the bush, and coming upon him from hollow logs and behind dark trees. His mind was always wandering to a verse he had found in the Bible: "Jerusalem hath grievously sinned; therefore she is removed: all that honored her despise her, because they have seen her nakedness: yea, she sigheth, and turneth backward."

"What does that mean, 'she sigheth and turneth backward'?" Otis wondered. "Could it be that she'll come back for me?" And with this thought in his head, he would tiptoe around cautiously, making sure that Lorraine Simmons was not waiting for him, crouched in some corner. Then he would slither away from whomever he was talking to, and run for home, never daring to turn around just once to see if anyone was following.

XVIII

The Misses Arcadia and Anarctica Cantrell never were particularly good friends of any of the Yellowhawk boys. The two old maids lived at the "other end" of the block, away from everybody, in a brown frame house with flat green shutters that flapped and fanned against the December winds and sagged under summer's heat. The two sisters (for how long had they been sisters, no one knew or dared ask), were like two peas in a pod—if one pea were yellow and the other green. Miss Arcadia had brown wispy hair, flat hazel eyes, and a tongue as soft as honey that had been used to catch a swarm of flies. Miss Anarctica, on the other hand, made no such pretenses. She was little and thin and looked as if she had been whittled out of a pipe stem. Her hair, if it had to be referred to, was generally described as "shingled." Her eyes were dry and severe, and her voice crackled and popped with the sternness that kept her withering body as straight as a gatepost.

They were old, and queer in their ways, and they kept to themselves. And, as has been said, they were never good friends of anyone. In a community as small as Yellowhawk, it wasn't possible not to classify people as Friends or Enemies. But Willynigh always hesitated to take the Misses Cantrell seriously enough to have to call them enemies, although he was scared to death of them, like all the other boys. But enemies meant people like Kenny R., who had stolen away all Willynigh's marbles while his big brothers yelled Fair Play, and his sister's cousin Rhoda, who was even more adamant in her dislike for him—she swiped his pants through a hole in their outhouse wall.

The Misses Cantrell, on the other hand, probably never bothered to classify anyone in their lives. To them, the entire neighborhood was formed of Workers. They were the two Queens. No one was a Drone. No one had a reason or an excuse to make himself a Drone. All were Dedicated Slaves to the Sister Queens who lived in that awful house and were queer in their ways and kept to themselves.

They used to lie in wait for the Yellowhawk boys—like Chester Heineman says the witches wait for churchgoers and turn them into cats—to make anyone they could catch go to work for them.

One fine spring day, Willynigh was off on a lark with his cousin T. Charlie, with a fishing pole in one hand and a can for worms in the other. They were just sauntering down the street, barefoot, blue jeaned, and dreamy eyed, thinking of the weeks and weeks of warm summer days stretched out before them, growing a little lazy and a bit neglectful, when all of a sudden—

"T. Charlie... yoo hoo, T. Charlie."

"Run, T. Charlie, run," Willynigh whispered, his heart in his throat.

"Yes'm," T. Charlie answered. "I can't do it, Willynigh, I can't. I'm too afraid they'll hex me. You know what Chester says..."

"Who's that with you, T. Charlie? He's too little to see. Is that Hannah's little boy? Is that you, Willy?"

And there Willynigh went, dragging his feet and pulling the can, so heavy now it seemed to weigh as much as a barrel of stick candy.

And there she was, Miss Arcadia, clucking him under the chin as if he were her pet rooster. "What a cute little thing. Willynigh, did you say? Why ever call him that?"

"Because he's nigh-on-to-a-grasshopper, he's so little," laughed T. Charlie, pulling himself up to his grand height of four foot three.

Willynigh began to cry.

Miss Arcadia's witch's heart started to thaw. "Don't cry, little Willynigh," she said sweetly, and he almost could see the honeyroll, thick and sweet and full of Willynigh flies, tossing about in her mouth. "Don't cry. Come in and Miss Arcadia will give you a nice cup of sassafras tea. You too, T. Charlie!"

So they left their fishing poles, cans, and anything else they happened to have, on the unswept block that made up the back stoop, following Miss Arcadia into the dark recesses that made up her polar-bear cave.

Willynigh was not really frightened. Excitement! he thought. At last I will see where they live, what it is like inside the Forbidden—for Hannah had never let him get close to the Misses Cantrell.

But T. Charlie shushed him right up. "Don't touch anything," he chirruped. "You'll get warts. And if you eat anything they give you, it'll come up in frog's legs."

Willynigh clutched his stomach. Were they going to be poisoned after all? He looked at Miss Arcadia—her back didn't look so foreboding to him as her front had. The softness puckering through her lilac dress in little tuckers of fat reminded him of his grandmother, whose fullness had always been a hideaway for him—he could bury himself in those cotton folds and shut out the light and the darkness of day.

"Oh, stop it!" she shrieked. "You nasty little boy!"

Whack! Down came her knuckles on Willynigh's fingers. "You pinched me."

T. Charlie nudged his friend. "I warned you."

"I didn't do anything."

"Never mind. Buck up. If you cry, the tears will freeze to your cheeks and we'll have to go to the drugstore to get liniment and wash them away."

So, Willynigh bucked up, and was lifted into a dirty white chair at an even dirtier table covered by an oilcloth (his mother Hannah kept a clean kitchen). On it were dishes and dishes of preserves—the preserves they made by intriguing little boys to pick plums and apples and berries and pears by the basketful.

Willynigh turned his head and stared at the picture of Jesus tacked to the newspapered wall.

"What would you like, Willynigh?"

He said nothing.

"I'm talking to ye."

"Nothing, thank you," Willynigh said then, remembering what Hannah had told him was polite in making a refusal.

"Nothing! Nothing! Look, little boy. Look at my jellies. Have what you will on a nice slab of homemade bread, with a little covering of butter, fresh churned. Not too much butter, though, you might grow up to be a fat little boy." And she turned her head away and cackled.

"What's this, Arcadia? Who've you dragged in now?" This came in the loud thrashing tones that reminded Willynigh of angry thunder, shouting down its curses on Hannah and him as it flooded out their garden that awful year, and left them with so little to eat that they gave him the name of Willynigh. Then, through the dusty curtains that made a door, came the sparse stick-like shadow of Miss Anarctica.

"How did she get that name?" Willynigh'd once asked T. Charlie.

"Wait till you see her," T. Charlie had said. "She'll remind you of something cold and frozen—she's like ice cakes floating under the river, floating to cover up the bodies of drowned fishes and men."

Willynigh shivered. He wanted to jump down and run, run, run to the little hut he and T. Charlie had built of grasses and sticks amid the grapevines, and furnished with mud dishes they swiped from Kenny R.'s sister. But T. Charlie punched him and he sat still.

She came on through the curtain, and stood there staring at the boys.

"Oh, yes, T. Charlie and Hannah's little boy, Willynigh," she said. Willynigh thought he saw a smile cross her face.

Impossible. No icicle ever smiled.

"They look hungry," said Miss Arcadia. "Don't you think a nice slice of bread and preserves would be good for them?"

"I imagine so. But they won't take it."

"Yes, they will," Miss Anarctica glared. "Won't you, boys?" Willynigh and T. Charlie turned numb and nodded.

"See. Now which preserves do you want?"

"Strawberry," said T. Charlie. "Please."

"Doesn't matter," Willynigh shook his head.

"Oh, but it does," said Miss Arcadia. "The choice of preserves is as important as one's horoscope. It brings about either a strawberry or cherry or blackberry morning."

Willynigh began to catch on.

"Plum, please," he said.

"My favorite, also," said Miss Arcadia.

Miss Anarctica had turned her back to them. She was fiddling with the stove. Then she bent double, her body still ramrod straight, and pulled out pans, and pans, and more pans.

"Fixin' to make more, I'll bet," whispered T. Charlie.

The boys took the round cups of sassafras tea, filled to the brim with fresh warm milk, and sipped as quickly as they could under Miss Arcadia's watchful eye. Then they put their hands in their laps and waited.

"More?" Miss Arcadia asked.

"No, thank you."

Miss Anarctica dropped her long wooden spoon and came across the room to the table. She helped lift them down—she got T. Charlie instead of Willynigh, thank heavens. Willynigh would have passed out if she had lain a hand on him.

Miss Arcadia helped walk them to the door. "You'll be back?" she said.

T. Charlie squirmed. Willynigh dug his foot in the warm dirt.

"Well, won't you?"

"I don't know," T. Charlie ventured. "Summer 'n' spring keep us mighty busy, you know."

"Oh? Too busy to stop by and see an old lady now and then? What about you, Willynigh?"

Willynigh stared up at her. She stared down at him. He saw her vacant eyes looking not at him, but at the little grasses shooting up beneath his feet. What do they mean to her, to make her smile? he wondered.

"Do spring and summer keep you busy, too, Willynigh? As busy as they keep Miss Anarctica and me, making preserves?"

Willynigh was only a little boy then. That's why they called him Willynigh. But he had a seventh sense, Hannah said. He could get the real meaning from things, and from people. And all of a sudden he got the real meaning from Miss Arcadia. She

wasn't a witch. She was only an old, old lady and very lonely...
wanting company almost as much as she wanted the fruits that
smelled so sweet under the summer sun. And here he was, a
little boy with many, many summers to look forward to—with
time enough to fish and play in grass houses and wade along the
river bank.

"Yes'm," Willynigh said slowly. "I'll be back."

T. Charlie's eyes bolted open.

"I'll bring you a basket of plums when I come, too. Your jelly
was awful good."

Then he turned and ran. T. Charlie ran, too, dangling his
fishing pole in the dirt. He ran the other way, shouting back,
"You're daft. You're as daft as she is. They got to you! I warned
you that they would, Willynigh!"

Willynigh slowed to a walk, shrugged his shoulders, and
went on down the road.

☙XIX☙

Mary Kinney's white muslin sheets had never felt as wet and heavy as the day she hung them out in the back lot to dry. "You'd think with all the wear we give 'em, they'd get light as fishnet," she grunted.

From the window of the trailer, her man Henry picked his teeth and watched her closely.

"They'll just get dirty again, flappin' up against the fence," he hollered.

"Says you." She reached hard for a clothes pin.

"The air's going' to be sooty today from the factory."

"Blowing all the way across the river from Carson? That's not likely."

"Just don't come wailin' to me that you've got to do the wash again."

"Oh, go on in," Mary said under her breath. "And don't stand there to pester me. I've got enough to do cooking all week long in a school cafeteria besides play sick nurse to as healthy a man as God ever put on this earth."

Henry, as if he had heard her, turned his back and jiggled his feet slightly.

Out in the yard, Mary could hear the refrigerator door snap.

It's nothing but food, Monday through Friday, she thought. "It's nothing but cheese sandwiches, chili, and apple–brown betty. Everybody reaching and grabbing and pushing for more. And now it's you on a Saturday morning. So get out of the ice box," she shouted aloud. "We've got just enough—there'll be no snacking until somebody goes for the groceries."

Henry shrugged his shoulders and sluffed back to his imitation-

leather-covered arm chair in the tiny living room. He propped
his feet on Mary's sewing stool and reached for last night's newspaper. The light was not good enough for him to make out the
print, so he had to push the floor lamp's drab shade back and
pull the glaring bulb directly over his left shoulder.

"What now, Lord," Mary sniffed, seeing the light flash on.
"Now he's wasting our electricity in the daytime. I never turn
the lights on. By heaven, it'll be the tube next."

She heard the faint musical sound of applause and laughter
that earmarked a quiz show, then saw the profile of Henry rocking himself back and forth, his big arms thrashing as he meticu-
lously adjusted sound, picture, lighting.

Mary sunk her wrinkled neck down into the collar of her
cleaning dress and, picking up the clothes basket, strode up the
steps into the kitchen. "Men," she muttered. "You'd think they'd
put their time to better use."

But then, a man like Henry? It was work, work, work, as hard
as he could. Henry was a man for shift duty. Henry was the
man for overtime. Henry was the man to lay over for a sick
buddy. Henry was a glutton for work. His big hairy arms slung a
hammer, his round muscled legs stood their weight on the concrete floor, supporting the heaving bulk of energy that worked,
worked, worked. His little lunch hour was his only break during
the eight-hour shift. He ate whatever Mary had fixed for him
and never complained. Usually there were only peanut butter and
jelly sandwiches and a thermos of lukewarm coffee that Mary,
the star cook of Yellowhawk, had thrown together, sputtering the
entire five minutes or so she spent at it, how she hated to be a
slave to a man's lunch box for twenty-five years.

Had Henry been a thinking man, he might have told her that
he had not found working to support her and trying to please her
the most rewarding thing he could have done. But he was not a
thinking man. And work was his escape. Good, hard, grueling
sweat-drawing work that wiped everything from his tiny mind
but the sound of that hammer clanging against steel; tremendous
steel, that bent and broke to the demands of his powerful hammer.

"Mary Kinney," her father had said to her when she was seventeen and a lovely girl. "Mary, you'll soon find out what kind of a man you're marrying. It'll be all work and no play for you."

She had left her father's house and learned the truth of his words. Not a single movie or church service had the man taken her to. Not one child had he given her. Only a life of penny pinching, even with her job to help out, and praying for better times.

"Before I die," she often said to herself at night as she scrubbed up the floor beneath the kitchen table, "before I die, I'm going places. Out of the kitchen, out of the cafeteria. I'm going to start by going to the movies. I want to go in every department store in Carson and shop until my arms are full of stuff, first- and second- and third-floor stuff, too—not basement bargains."

Mary Kinney had big plans. She kept herself prim and neat. The rosy fleshiness of youth had fallen off and left her thin and bony, so that she looked good in a straight skirt and sweater, she told herself as she primped before the bathroom mirror. She kept her hair curly with home permanents, and she always creamed her face before bed. She saw to it that there was enough money left from the groceries and rent to buy that cream.

"Who knows?" she often thought. "I may meet me a handsome man someday, after Henry goes. I may be marrying again."

And she would pinch her cheeks and grin into the mirror.

But if Mary Kinney ever took another husband, it would be different sort from Henry. She wanted someone little, who would not wear the upholstery thin from the fat little rolls on the back of his neck and the weight of his arms and thighs. She wanted someone who would not fill her ashtrays with cigar butts and her neatly scrubbed wastecans with beer bottles. She wanted a man who would drain out his tub and turn down the rug when it flopped up at the corner, and she wanted a man who would not forget to call her Lovey now and then. "Lovey, you've got to quit your job. I won't have you slaving over a hot stove every day. Lovey, just stay at home and be beautiful for me when I get back from the office."

"I've worked," Mary thought. "I deserve it. I deserve the good life. Others get it, why shouldn't I?"

She dusted around Henry, making him lift his big feet and

legs, making him lean forward and backward so she could remove every particle of dust that had settled on her furniture.

Henry did her bidding, keeping his eyes on the TV screen all the while.

Then Mary turned off the light and told him he didn't need it if he was going to watch TV.

"Turn it back," he said. "I can't see without it."

"Sweet Jesus." Mary switched the light back on and went to pound the rug with her broom and wipe the drawers of her standtable.

"Come sit with me," Henry said suddenly. "Come sit down and watch."

Mary Kinney turned to him, a look of surprise spreading across her disapproving face. "Henry Kinney," she snapped, "you know I don't take to my chair in the daytime."

"Oh, Lovey," he grinned. "Just this once. It's a funny program. And I'm on vacation."

Mary stomped out of the living room and went to plumping the bed that Henry had leaned against.

Her husband shrugged his shoulders and went back to laughing at the quiz-show contestants.

"Now why did he say a fool thing like that?" Mary asked herself. "He knows I don't approve of that sort of thing. Only having the weekends at home the way I do, I need to work every minute to keep this place clean."

Vacation! His vacation, not hers. She never had any vacation from the cleaning, no less the cooking, shopping, mending. Her neighbors said she should take it easier. They said there wasn't that much to do, for two old people living in a trailer. Well, maybe they didn't find much to do, but her hours were never idle. "No, sir," Mary frowned. "I don't while my time away. I've got work to do."

She was surprised about Henry's vacation. He had never taken one before. Not in the twenty-five years they had been married. It was always work, work, work. Henry at the shops, Mary at school and home. All day long, they labored in their separate ways, and at night they slept in the same bed, but as far apart from each other as they could lie. Then this year he decided to take a vacation—right in the middle of her school year—and to spend it here at home. For a week she had had him on her hands, waiting for her to come home, tagging at her heels, wanting this, wanting that, pretending he did not feel well, when she was too busy to talk to him. She had finally agreed to sit by him in the evenings, or even to walk down the street with him.

"It's spring, Mary Kinney, and we've got old," he had said. "Let's take time out to be young just this week."

She shook her head. What had got into the man? They'd gone their own ways too long to try to mend them. It was best to let things lie the way they had settled.

In the kitchen, she stirred up batter for hot bread and laid the pork chops out to be warming. "How about a fried chicken?" Henry had hinted. "My mom used to fix the best fried chicken when we were at home together on Sundays."

"Well," Mary thought, "I'm not your mom. And I don't have time to fool with a chicken. These chops'll just have to do. Besides, it's not Sunday, either."

The kitchen window began to rattle, and she glanced up. A strong wind was blowing, and dark rain clouds were gathering.

"Mary," Henry called from the living room, "Your washing's about to get wet."

"My washing!" she thought. "It's both of us who uses those things, Henry." But she slammed the back door irritably and rushed out into the lot, saying nothing.

The white sheets were batting against the fence, dirtying themselves on the sooty grime that had collected there. One pillowcase had already been blown to a pile of bricks on the ground. With a moan, Mary began picking up the laundry, pulling down what was left on the line.

The kitchen door blew open, and she got a glimpse of Henry, standing in the doorway.

"Mary," he called. "Mary."

She turned her back. "I don't want to see his face," she thought. "I don't want to see that gloating look he'll have. I don't want to hear him say 'I told you so.'" She went about her work.

When she heard the door slam, she relaxed. "He's gone," she thought. She waited a moment, then she started back inside.

Henry was lying on the kitchen floor. His eyes were open, and his hands were clutching at his chest. But he wasn't breathing.

"Henry?" Mary said. "Henry?" She touched him with her index finger. "Henry?"

She peeped into the living room. He had overturned a lamp and kicked up a rug on his way to the kitchen. The freshly waxed floor was scraped, as if he had dragged his heels across it.

"Why, Henry," Mary said again. "Are you all right? No, you're not, are you? Henry, are you dead?"

Henry did not answer.

Mary peered at him carefully. "Why, Henry Kinney, you look as if you've been laughing," she said. "What was so funny?"

Henry's lips were curled in a smile.

"I guess it was me out there getting in the clothes," Mary thought. "I guess that's what it was. You told me that would happen, but I wouldn't listen. Well, you were right, but you can't hear me tell you so."

She stepped over Henry's body to put a pork chop back into the refrigerator. "We won't need both of them," she said aloud, "seeing that there's only going to be one for dinner tonight."

Then she went into the living room, to set up the lamp and straighten the rug before she went to get help.

XX

I'm not sure that I ever knew what freedom was or that I ever will know what it is. I don't think that's something a person ever does find out, really. A lot of people spend so much time thinking about freedom and philosophizing over what it is and whether they have it or not that they lose their inner peace and understanding and just end up quarreling with themselves and trying to figure out why they can't have all the answers just because they were bright enough to think of the questions. So they even forget the issue. I can't help thinking that's funny.

I've had a lot of freedom, I think. A lot more than most people —perhaps because I wasn't so sure about things at the time and so I tended to take them just for what they were, and not ask too many questions. I don't know, maybe not—it's just an idea.

I think a lot lately. But I don't think too much about earth-shaking, serious things. I think about the years that have passed and the ones that are to come. And when I do think about them, I try to connect them and build a bridge between them. I try not to remember the bad times, the bitter parts, but only remind myself that the flowers were beautiful in the April when this or that happened, and then I wonder if spring will be lush and green this year or if March will come in so cold and blustery that no young thing will have a chance for proper survival. And the autumn when I had the wreck becomes a late autumn that was cold and sad but I can still remember how splendid the trees were in their bleakness and how I hurt with understanding when I looked at their bare black outlines against the gray morning sky because I felt like a dark bare silhouette, too, something propped up by an unseen force and held there and stared at. And I know that this autumn I'll dread seeing the trees that way. But I'll make myself look at them and take pity on their bareness and I will rejoice with them when winter brings fresh snow to cover them over until the spring gives back their green.

This autumn I will have a baby and I will know what it is like to have brought life into this world as well as to have taken it away. I'll probably think even less about serious things then as I go about taking care of my child and helping her grow up in my world. I'll want to take a lot of time to teach her the things she'll need to know. I don't want her to have to learn everything the hard way, the way I sometimes catch myself thinking that I did. Then freedom will mean for me the chance to sit down for a minute and be by myself while the baby's sleeping or slip out for a movie with Jack some night when my sister is watching the baby. It won't be a big deal, or will it? Will that make me feel more real and more important and more alive than I do when I sit around thinking about why I was born and who I am, and why the things that have happened to me have happened?

Sometimes Jack tells me very gently that I am playing roles; he tells me that I will get tired of being a full-time housewife and mother, just the way I got tired of being a full-time widow and admitted that there was a lot of life left in me and married him. Jack would never be unkind, he only says things like that to tease me and let me know that he thinks a lot about me and understands. Do I think that much about him? Perhaps, as I become less self-centered, I'll be able to turn towards him more completely. After all, do I understand the little feelings and fears he has buried down deep inside him? I don't know. But I want to, and I try. That's a start.

But I think Jack's right about my playing roles. After all, I played the seventeen-year-old girl just dying to get married, then I was the unhappy wife, then I was the guilty widow after the accident. That's when I really started thinking so much about freedom, right after the accident when I was alive and he wasn't. I kept wondering why. I kept asking myself why we had even made the drive, why I was driving, why I was the one who had lived. All the questions we can't help asking ourselves over and over even though we know there will never be any answers. It was the beginning of my self-torture, the beginning of my awakening and then, with Jack, the start of my gradual understanding.

And then I went to Yellowhawk. How can you ever say what it's like to suddenly feel your eyes coming open, your heart jumping up in your throat, your very body alive and eager to work and give yourself to people who are there with you and alive back at you and important to you for no reason at all. Just because they are, and there are no reasons for that, either.

I found out as much about freedom there as I ever will understand. It was the way I felt as I walked through the morning wind from my car in through the doors of that red-brick school building. With my hair blowing in the wind and my hands tingling as I held books or flowers or jars of tadpoles or just a dream or two that had carried over from the day before. It was the way I felt when I looked into *their* faces and they looked back into mine, little children born and bred to their country ways, to their lives of solitude and too often poverty but to a deep understanding of themselves and others. They gave me self-respect and love and I tried to show them that I understood. I tried to look at them with love and let them see that love and self-understanding and even—for the first time in my life—pride written all over my face and more than that alive and radiating from my body. Freedom, yes. Freedom to look about you and learn from others, see their achievements and their errors. But not judge. Only look and see, and understand. Only be sympathetic, show pride or pity, but not judge. Try to understand. As they tried to understand me and taught me to understand myself.

Yes, I think that Jack is right. There will come a time when I am ready to go back there. Maybe not because I get tired of being the fulltime mother and housewife—for how could I not be a mother every minute of my life? I already feel that this child inside me belongs to me and to my world and that I belong to her forever: we have no freedom to be severed apart from each other, nor do we want it! And I will always belong here in this house that Jack built and brought me to. It will always be my home, my place to make beautiful and fill with the love of life I want so badly now to share. But yes, there will be a time when the need for something else becomes so great that I will return to the best part of my past. I'll go back to Yellowhawk and take up where I left off. I'll go back to new children sitting at new desks, but it will all be old to me. A good world that my new sense of freedom lets me enter into willingly, and with a little sense of amusement for things past. And who knows, maybe these new children will be the children of the girls and boys who sat there before. And maybe they'll go home to their mothers and daddies and say guess what, my new teacher is Rhoda Miller, and their parents will either have forgotten or they will smile and remember. When that time comes, I'll be ready.

THE END

❧ABOUT THE AUTHOR❧

Jane Stuart is the daughter of Jesse, noted American poet, novelist, short-story writer, farmer, and teacher. Jane was born in eastern Kentucky and grew up there in a world that combined farm life and a love of literature. Inevitably asked whether her father has had any influence on her writing, she says emphatically, "Yes. He was always interested in what I said or thought or put down on paper, but never tried to suggest I do things his way. He understood that what I expressed was the world I saw through my own eyes. I have followed in my father's footsteps, but I have gone my own way."

Possessor of a *magna cum laude* A.B., two M.A.'s (in classical languages and in Italian), and a Ph.D. in Italian Literature, Jane is the wife of Julian C. Juergensmeyer, and the mother of sons Conrad and Erik.